Grace's Seasons

Bryan, Best Coach Ever.
May you Let Love,
Peace & Joy Be your
Constant Companion.

God Bless you

Shay

6/14/22

"NJoy"

Grace's Seasons

Book 2 in the
Artist Wife series

SHARRON BEDFORD-VINES

Copyright © 2022 Sharron Bedford-Vines.

All rights reserved. No part of this book may be used or reproduced by any means, graphic, electronic, or mechanical, including photocopying, recording, taping or by any information storage retrieval system without the written permission of the author except in the case of brief quotations embodied in critical articles and reviews.

Archway Publishing books may be ordered through booksellers or by contacting:

Archway Publishing
1663 Liberty Drive
Bloomington, IN 47403
www.archwaypublishing.com
844-669-3957

Because of the dynamic nature of the Internet, any web addresses or links contained in this book may have changed since publication and may no longer be valid. The views expressed in this work are solely those of the author and do not necessarily reflect the views of the publisher, and the publisher hereby disclaims any responsibility for them.

Any people depicted in stock imagery provided by Getty Images are models, and such images are being used for illustrative purposes only. Certain stock imagery © Getty Images.

Scriptures taken from the King James Version of the Bible.

ISBN: 978-1-6657-1777-9 (sc)
ISBN: 978-1-6657-1776-2 (hc)
ISBN: 978-1-6657-1778-6 (e)

Library of Congress Control Number: 2022901031

Print information available on the last page.

Archway Publishing rev. date: 04/14/2022

Contents

Season 1	Dreams and Realities	1
Season 2	Family Does Matter	43
Season 3	Changed Attitudes	89
Season 4	Ambitious Encounters	105
Season 5	Shaping Patterns	135
Season 6	Unfathomable Disclosures	167
Season 7	The Truth Sets You Free	197
Season 8	In Due Season	227
Season 9	Defining Moments	257

To everything there is a season and a time
to every purpose under the heaven.

—Ecclesiastes 3:1

In Dedication:

Cleveland Robert Bedford (Loving Father 1929-2006)
Donald Eugene Bedford (Beloved Brother 1949 -2014)
Martha Hurse (Precious Friend 1953-2018) "It Is Well"

Acknowledgments

I'm Grateful and Thankful to my Lord and Savior Jesus Christ, from whence cometh my help. Thanks to my talented and supportive husband, Roederick, for inspirational ideas and stunning images throughout the book. The Archway Publishing Team. Editors, W. Calvin Anderson and Abrafi S. Sanyika. This seasons "Angels in Disguise" (Ameerah Akowah, The Rose of Sharon Ministries Team (Linda J. Turner, Donnie Rose Smith, Bobbi Rozann Broome, Ashley Ellis, Raina Green, Karen Turner, Fayth Turner and Devyn Marie Vierling).

I'm Grateful and Thankful to the Titus Women in my life: Fannie Doss, Barbara Hill, Ella Rose Ferguson and Muessetta Wise. To the women who impacted many seasons of my life (too numerous to name).

I'm Grateful and Thankful to my Family: Secret Sauce, Siblings Dennis Bedford, Joann Bedford, Frances Renee Wilcoxon, Trudy Bedford, Craig Bedford, Crystal Bedford, numerous nieces, nephews, and greats; the Bedford's, the Roby Nation, and the Vines' Family.

I'm Grateful and Thankful to all followers of the Artist Wife Series. I pray this story ignites faith, love, joy, and sparks creativity in your heart.

N-Joy

Sharron

SEASON 1
Dreams and Realities

CHAPTER

1

The Celebration

Grace had always loved Columbus Circle in New York City. It was a prestigious landmark connection on the West Side to most of New York's treasures. She always enjoyed sightseeing the larger corporate headquarters of Midtown Manhattan, Rockefeller Center, the Broadway theater district, the Hudson River, horse carriages, grand hotels, and Central Park. Robert's Restaurant was one of her favorite hot spots. When she arrived with her special guests, it was filled with laughter. The waitress led Grace's party of eight to their seats—Grace, her husband, Wellington, and her friends Ellona Robie, Dr. Monica Wolf, Tyler Hamilton, Tracey Vinson, Georgie Houston, and Carlos Ramos, an accomplished detective who specialized in crimes involving fine art.

After ordering their meals, Wellington proposed a toast. "Let me be the first to congratulate the Angels in Disguise team." He clinked his champagne glass with the others and placed a gentle kiss on Grace's lips.

"Thank you. Thank you. Thank you," said Grace, beaming with excitement. "This breakthrough could not have happened without God's help, first. And second, not without the knowledge and expertise of my awesome team of Dr. Monica, Tracey, and Georgie. We would not have developed the trade secret for the LAI." LAI referred to Liquid Art Intelligence.

"Hear, hear," they said, raising their glasses.

"Whew! It's been tough living with an artist during the development process," Wellington said. He smiled and wiped his brow in a mocked fashion.

"Ha-ha," Grace replied. She laughed and jokingly pushed his shoulder. "Like I've said many times before, *it's a relationship you wouldn't understand.*" They laughed in unison.

"All teasing aside, I'm really proud of you for following your vision to create something unique that will help so many," Wellington said.

"Thank you, my dear. We celebrate today, but the real work begins now to catch the art thieves," Grace said. "This tool is on the cutting edge of differentiating true, original art from the counterfeit." Grace raised her glass again.

"A toast to taking the art criminals down," Dr. Monica Wolf chimed in.

Glasses clinked again.

The waiter approached the table with a bottle of Cristal. "The couple across the room sends their congratulations to you," the waiter announced.

Everyone looked toward the table in the back and raised their glasses to the anonymous couple.

"I wonder who they are," Grace said in between sips. "Nobody outside our private circle is privy to our celebration."

"They probably just want to get in on the fun," Wellington guessed.

Monica raised her eyebrows. "Or maybe they recognize you and Wellington. You are pretty famous."

"Nevertheless, that's more champagne for us," Ty said quickly.

Detective Ramos remained silent, but he noticed Ty's changed demeanor and his fidgeting hands. The detective kept his eye on the couple who had sent the champagne. When they rose to leave, he excused himself from the table. He approached the hostess desk to find out their names. She searched the log and gave him the name—Sergeant.

"Is there a last name?"

She smiled. "That's all I have."

~

Olu Adebayo and Kiko Yamamoto hurried to the waiting black limousine.

"You got the information we need?"

"I'm working on it," Kiko responded.

"Do not tell me that you are working on it. Make it happen! And look at me when I am talking to you," he said in a frustrated tone.

Kiko's mind grew fuzzy as she decided the best reply. "In due season, we'll have all we need. I'm in like that," Kiko replied sarcastically. She pulled off her dark shades and threw her long blonde wig to the floor of the limo.

By the time Detective Ramos reached the door of the restaurant, the limo had sped away, preventing him from getting a clear look at the generous but mysterious couple.

CHAPTER 2

Deep Roots Talk

One Year Prior to the Celebration

Grace sat at her vanity, looking in the mirror while putting on her makeup. She felt like she was seeing right through herself and looking into her own world. She had an epiphany as she thought about how her life had turned around over the years. It seemed like just yesterday when she was crying over the loss of so many diverse things. She had cried because she thought Wellington had been killed in a plane accident. She had cried because she'd lost their baby during this time. She had even lost hope of ever being considered a significant artist. God had certainly changed things. Wellington was indeed alive and blessed throughout his recovery. They were blessed with another child—a daughter, Radiance, who was now fourteen. They had also welcomed Wellington's son, Javier, who'd had come to live with them after his mom died. He'd come while battling a health crisis, but that was long ago. He was now a tall, handsome nineteen-year old. *To look now at all of it is really a beautiful thing,* she thought.

∼

Grace smiled to herself, remembering the day that Dr. Monica told her Wellington was still alive. She remembered their reunion on that beautiful sunny day in New York. She knew their greatest adversity in the past would be their biggest challenge going forward. Getting their marriage back on track was still of paramount importance. She realized, after an inner search, that her downfall was her intrinsic desire to have her own individual artistic expression. It was a painful lesson and a revelation that led her to change her ways, as well as to reconnect with God. Their marital relationship was restored. The demand for Wellington's art increased, which led to greater international recognition.

The lingering area of concern after Wellington's plane crash in Geneva, Switzerland, many years ago was his health. Upon his return to New York, his physician, Dr. Patel, recommended that he slow his teaching and travel schedules. Wellington's thoughts were different. He had been away so long from his studio that he needed to make up for lost time. Grace's concern had reached a level for a serious talk with him.

∼

"Wellington, the school is growing by leaps and bounds. Don't you think it's time to add more teachers? You can't keep doing everything yourself," Grace said.

"I think we've been doing OK." He turned to look at Grace. "By the look on your face, I can tell there is more to this conversation. What's your real concern, honey?"

"Your health, for one. I know we have money to hire more

teachers, but you want to teach all the classes. You can't keep up this pace!"

"What do you want me to do, woman?" he said. He made a gesture of listening with just one ear.

She turned him around. "Stop playing. I am serious, Wellington. Malcolm Jenkins is the perfect teacher to hire. He taught your classes a few times when you were in Switzerland and London, and he understands your vision. Are you listening?"

"Yes, I hear you. That's not a bad idea. After all, he was one of my top students."

"Ty Hamilton donated money to this school to make sure we had the best. He believes in you. All the students know Malcolm and like him. He is an accomplished associate professor at Columbia University and a PhD candidate, as well. You could cut your days and hours in half and let him teach some of the classes. You've made a great impact on his future as an artist. It will give him more experience and give you more creative time. And time for me, too."

"I guess I never thought about it that way. And I know I owe you and need to give you more time. You seem all in favor of him for some reason."

"That's because you need the rest, and he's a dedicated teacher."

"If it means that much to you, I can do that. I will give him a call."

"The two of us have managed this business by ourselves for years. We have to do things smarter, or we will wear ourselves out," Grace reminded him.

"You are right, dear. We deserve more downtime together. I'll call him," Wellington agreed.

"I will appreciate having you around for many more years. I do not want to be without you again. Keep in mind what the doctors suggested for your health. You are not doing it as well as you could," she gently scolded him.

"I know. I promise I'll try harder, but it's not easy. You know how the creative mode comes to us. We get on a roll and can't stop working. It's addictive!"

"I understand. But our family needs you. I need you."

"OK. OK. I get the message," he said, frustrated. "I thought my mom didn't live here."

"I'm your helpmate, and I know I get on your case like a mother would, but sometimes it is hard to separate the two. Ask any wife!"

"OK. I promise I'll talk to Malcolm right after the school dedication event tomorrow."

"That's my man," Grace said gently, rubbing his back. "I know. I'm being bossy again, right? Tell me again—your mother doesn't live here." Grace laughed and waved her fist.

He smiled. "I love when you own up to that."

Wellington Holmes

CHAPTER 3

Wellington Holmes Art Academy Dedication

It was a sunny Monday afternoon as Wellington and Grace prepared for the three o'clock grand opening of the new Wellington Holmes Art Academy facilities.

"What's bothering you?" Wellington asked as they pulled into their reserved parking space. "I thought you were looking forward to this day."

"It's me. That's what's bothering me. I cannot wrap my head around this. It is a bit overwhelming," Grace replied.

"We've been anticipating this for the past three years. The crowd is here, students are excited, and the school is paid for in full. What more could we ask for?" Wellington replied.

"It's not that I'm ungrateful. It seems all too good to be true. I sincerely hope that this is the end of our troubled story."

"Didn't we ask God for this? Didn't it take faith to get this far?" Wellington pinched Grace's smooth brown cheeks. He gently moved her hair away from her eyes and looked squarely into them as he kissed her.

"The reason I'm telling you is so that you'll pray for me." She tried to keep the fear out of her voice.

"I always pray for you. You know my heart is synchronized with yours." He kissed her again, softly, and engaged her full and luscious lips even longer. "I guess I have questions too," he admitted.

"Like what?"

"This building is expensive. Ty and his partners easily dropped $10 million for this project. Why did they do that for us?"

"You already know the answer to that. He has money, and, as a philanthropist, he has a heart for the endowment of the arts."

"I know you're right. It must be my emotions, or it could be the medicine. I don't seem to have the same joy or inspiration for the goals I set for myself," Wellington replied.

"You have been through a great deal. I know this celebration is emotional after all that happened. Look at both of us doubting this moment. What is wrong with us? The larger blessing is that the movie studios are vying for the rights to your story. That can't be anybody but God!" Grace declared, pointing her finger upward in the air. "The enemy is trying to plant negative thoughts in our minds because he doesn't want us to enjoy this moment of blessings. Our season for God's blessings is now. Let's claim it!"

"I know we are blessed. We are fortunate to have a state-of-the-art education facility, a sculpture and draftsmanship studio, media and music studios, administration rooms, sports complex, library, cafeteria, computer labs, and virtual learning classrooms and conference rooms. This was my vision, and I am happy it came to fruition." He lifted his hands in the air. "But that is not the issue. My question to God is, why me? Why did He save me in the plane crash? Is there something more He wants me to do for Him?" Wellington asked.

"I believe He does have years of special things for you to do. Both of us seek alignment with all of God's vision. We hold the future of many young artists in our hands. God, in all His goodness, has entrusted us to fulfill His mission and bless others. Let's not worry about that right now. We have a celebration to attend." Grace winked and reassured him by squeezing his hand. Wellington stepped out of Grace's gleaming Black Mercedes S500. He opened Grace's door and extended his hand. They approached the side door of the stage.

"Ladies and gentlemen, please put your hands together and help me welcome Wellington and Grace Holmes," the announcer said. The crowd went wild with applause. They waved as they stepped to the podium and Wellington quieted the crowd with a hand gesture.

"Thank you, everyone, for joining us as we dedicate this beautiful facility. It warms our hearts to see how much you care. We know that without God, this day would not have been possible. We also know that we could not have achieved this without all of you, and we thank you for your support. A special shout-out to our patron, Ty Hamilton, and his staff for his tremendous multimillion-dollar financial support. We thank you again for supporting the vision and stepping up to equip future generations with the means to achieve their artistic dreams. Students, we promise to give you the tools that you will need to be successful and the life skills to thrive in this world. Thank you again for coming. Please enjoy the celebration."

Mayor Bill de Blasio greeted them at the bottom of the stairs as they left the stage. Grace's mom, Ruth, looking elegant in an off-white pantsuit, hugged her. Standing next to Ruth was their assistant Marcella, and Grace's friend Ellona. Dr. Monica Wolf came up from behind and touched Grace on the shoulder, and they hugged with great joy.

"It's so good to see you. I wasn't sure you'd make it, with the multiple developments at the Centers for Disease Control keeping you busy. I thought work would hold you up in Switzerland."

Monica smiled. "My schedule has been crazy. We've been working around the clock on a new vaccine for infectious respiratory diseases with few breaks. Ty made sure I took time out for this but also for my own health. I'm so glad I'm here to celebrate this moment with both of you. You look great, Grace. How is Wellington doing? He looks tired."

"The days leading up to this celebration have been overwhelming, and he hasn't been getting enough sleep."

"Dr. Patel still requires a quarterly visit to keep a check on his health. I hope he is obeying his orders and not working as much."

Grace winced. "That's an offline conversation we need to have. How are things with you?"

"Going well. Girl, I am so busy at the CDC. You know that I am dedicated to helping others through the human sciences. Since we developed the vaccine for the Salton Sea disease, which you know is related to your son Javier's condition, my phone has not stopped ringing. You can't imagine the number of cases in California and other regions that are caused by dirty, polluted waters. My work as an epidemiologist is in high demand. We have to look out for the next global threat."

"We are so grateful that your lab discovered the vaccine that will extend not only Javier's life but all of those located near the US and Mexico border. Environmentally, the Salton Sea was the largest body of water in that region of California and Mexico, and the dust left behind is dangerous for a lot of people," Grace replied.

Monica added. "Because I live in Switzerland, the Swiss media want to be the first to interview me about the lifesaving vaccine that helped Javier. In addition, they know we are close friends, and they want a feature story about you and Wellington—the premiere artists and rising movie stars."

"I'll check our schedules and see if we can make that happen and maybe do some business while we're there. By the way, you also look good."

"Thank you. I couldn't be happier." Monica beamed. "Ty is a wonderful man. I never believed that I would find love again. And to think I was resisting him."

"Girl, that is what I was talking about. Loving someone deeply and giving of yourself may seem like a risk, but you found the courage. You did it!"

"No, girl, God did it!" Monica smiled and displayed the teardrop diamond on her left hand. "He proposed!"

"Oh, my goodness!" Grace exclaimed, checking out Monica's ring. "I know you said yes."

"You better believe it. After all these years, there's no way I'm going to let this good catch get away."

"I'm happy for you two."

"It's been a learning experience to trust him." Monica lowered her eyes.

"Have you set a date?"

"Not yet."

"Let me know. I would love to throw a bridal shower for you here in New York, where your friends can celebrate this wonderful occasion."

"I will." Monica's eyes sparkled. "Thank you."

Grace glanced over at Ty and saw him talking to Detective Ramos, Wellington, and a sharply dressed good-looking man. They ended their conversation and walked toward Grace and Monica.

"Congratulations, you two." Ty hugged Wellington and Grace.

"Thanks. I understand congratulations are in order for you, and Monica as well," Grace said.

Wellington shook Ty's hand tightly and held on to it for a long time. "We are thankful for your generous donation, my friend."

"Man, it's my pleasure. Education and the arts go hand in hand. Now that things are rolling at the school, I guess you'll be getting back on the road soon, which brings me to my next point. Grace, I already introduced my friend Max to Wellington. Now, I want you and the others to meet the finest African American agent in the world, Maxwell Shelton."

They all shook hands. Maxwell lingered a moment when he shook Ellona's hand.

"You can call me Max. It is nice to meet you," he said to all, though he looked directly into Ellona's eyes.

Ellona was slightly taken aback by both his gaze and attention.

"I know you two talked about hiring a new agent. Max handles requests for the top art collectors in Hollywood and in New York," Ty bragged.

"Impressive!" Wellington said, and Grace nodded in agreement.

"I suggest you set a time to sit down and talk and decide if he's a good fit."

"Sure. I guess you've heard how Grace's career has blossomed," Wellington said proudly, pulling Grace closer. Grace blushed profusely.

Max nodded. "I heard and have been following her career. Congratulations! If given the opportunity, I would love to set up some shows for you."

"We'll give it some thought." Grace turned towards Wellington.

"Max, how long will you be in New York?" Wellington asked.

"For a few more days. My schedule is flexible. Give me a call, and we can set something up." He handed Wellington his card.

"Sounds like a plan. Ty, we need to plan dinner with you and Monica before y'all leave town," Wellington said.

"I'll make that happen. Listen, folks, I have to run to a meeting." Ty shook Wellington's hand.

"Nice meeting all of you. I'll look forward to your call." Max tipped his hat to Ellona, and she returned a broad smile.

Grace bumped up against her shoulder, chuckling discreetly. "Ellona, I think you have an admirer."

"Damn, what a fine physical specimen!" Ellona followed him with her eyes. "I'm going to have to get him to come to my spa and treat him to my Ellona's Special." She winked at Grace.

Detective Ramos walked toward them, smiling.

"Congratulations, you two," he said to Wellington and Grace. I see that Ty Hamilton and his investors set you up royally," Detective Ramos said.

"Yes, they did, and we are grateful."

Detective Ramos did not reply.

"What's new in your world?" Wellington asked.

"You know, art investigations never cease. Private collectors, museums, and auction houses are always targeted by even more sophisticated criminals. They are disturbing everybody's peace—especially mine." He chuckled and scratched his head. "The international art trade is complex. It's indeed a new world order. We are investigating several fine art insurance frauds. Detective Fernando Mendez is working with me on this. He has twenty-five years of experience in working with museums."

"That sounds like job security to me." Wellington smiled.

"The Swiss government has teamed up with the Japanese government on another matter that is more flagrant."

"What matter is that, may I ask?" Wellington inquired.

"Someone is taking original art painted by the Masters and reproducing them to sell counterfeits."

"Really?"

"It appears to be a New York connection, but it's still too early to add up all the connections. We are whittling down the players as we speak."

"Man, that sounds like a daunting task. It's scary what people are doing these days. We wouldn't want anything like that to happen to our originals," Wellington said.

"I'm keeping my nose to the ground on this one, and I surely will keep you posted."

"We appreciate it. Good to see you again." Grace smiled.

"I'll be in touch," said Detective Ramos.

CHAPTER

4

The Dream

Grace and Monica walked through the Contemporary Art Space at the famous E-Zee Gallery, lined with exquisite original oil paintings. They giggled and pumped a high-five as they viewed the paintings and envisioned the Liquid Art Intelligence security-mapping signatures on the back of the paintings. The crowd in attendance was interested in hearing about solutions to protect their masterpieces and specific ways to track down the original forces behind the pervasive incidents of art theft. Members of the Artist Wife Organization were present and seated in the front row. As the curator introduced Grace, she stepped on the platform to demonstrate how the tool functioned.

A strange man dressed in all black stealthily pressed his way through the crowd to get a better view of her. Observing her beauty and shapely legs, he wondered how she could be so bold and yet naïve as to think she would stop the phenomenal influx of criminals that infiltrated his art biosphere. The diverse and eclectic crowd clapped enthusiastically after Grace's passionate speech about the technological aspects of LAI's unique tracking signatures, fine art asset protection, and fraud prevention. Wiping his dripping brow, the stranger placed his hands in his deep jacket pockets, and pulled out a deadly aerosol solution. He pointed a cannister to the ceiling and then released a projectile of powder into the air that caused everyone in the crowd to choke, cough, and disperse, with many falling to the floor. He turned toward Grace and winked at her before pumping his fist in the air, as if to signify a victory. Then he vanished.

In that instant, Grace froze at the recognition of this adversary. A sudden, strong, uncontrollable spirit lifted her down off the stage. She kicked and tried to catch herself before falling, but her arms and legs were like rubber as she floated in the air. She heard God say, *This is the way you should go*, as she fell off her soft, fluffy bed.

Wellington sat up and rolled over to see her face down on the floor. Grace rocked up to a sitting position and pulled herself back into bed.

Wellington's eyes were wide. "What just happened?"

"There was an evil force in my dream that disrupted a large event, and I was trying to get away. Many times, when I wake up from a dream, I don't always understand it. This time is different. I believe it's prophetic."

"Prophetic? You think every dream is spiritual."

"No, not all dreams, but this one is different. When I woke up, I had the solution."

"The solution to what?"

"You know my passion for art and doing something about those crooks who are making a living by stealing from the artists. In my dream, God made it crystal clear how to put a stop to all of it."

"I'm listening."

"Wellington, I believe God gave me an idea."

"Oh boy. Here we go." He smirked.

"Stop laughing at me." She pouted and poked him. "I'll only tell you about my dream if you promise not to shoot it down."

"Go ahead, sweetheart. I promise! Now that I'm awake, you have my undivided attention. Tell me the premonition and the prophecy." He puffed up the pillows behind him.

"I believe God showed me a device that can be created."

"What kind of device?" he asked.

"I don't know exactly. All I know is that in the dream, I was introducing a new fine art security tool to a crowd of people, and the encrypted identification was on the back of the demonstration painting. Monica and my girls from the Artist Wife Organization were there too. It had to do with an acid-free liquid and a rare kind of tracking signature in the back of the painting."

"What's an acid-free liquid signature?"

"I know it doesn't make sense. I didn't see it clearly in the dream. It's something that formed in my spirit sometime between the dream and waking up. I cannot explain it. That is just like God. Things don't always make sense at first. But in my dream, I saw the item on the back of a painting."

"It sounds complicated."

"It probably is."

"Who do you think can help with that?" he asked.

"Monica was in the dream with me. So that may be a clue. Since she is a scientist, she's good at research and development and can provide advice on the acid-free portion. At least it's a starting point."

"I like the sound of it. In fact, I don't know of anything of this nature, but I know it's needed in our industry to identify original art from a counterfeit. What would you call it?" he asked.

"I heard 'Liquid Art Intelligence.' We could shorten it, and call it LAI," said Grace.

"I think you may have come up with something unique. I hope that it's not something that would put you in danger. It's been difficult for the museums and galleries to track their artwork, as well as for the artists who spent long hours laboring over their craft," said Wellington. "This is way out of my league, for sure. Girl does your mind ever stop?"

"I sometimes wish it could slow down." She smiled. "I'll call Monica later today and run it past her while it is still fresh in my mind. But there is more."

"What else, dear?"

"Now that I'm considering graduate school, this may be a good subject for my thesis. You never know where this could lead. You know how much I want to give back to the community and leave a legacy," Grace said.

"If that is your desire, you know I'm behind you," he said, kissing her softly. "You always have a good plan. That's why I married you." He hugged her.

Grace released herself from his embrace. "I thought you said you married me because of my uncommon courage?"

"I believe you are still working on that," he teased, pushing a pillow in her face. "Since we're awake, let me tell you what's on my mind."

"My ears are open, Professor." She cupped her hand around her left ear.

"Lately, you haven't shown the same interest in my work as you used to. What's up with that?" he asked.

"Oh, now look who's talking. The shoe is on the other foot. The Artist Husband is feeling left out. I seem to remember those days myself." She cuddled him and kissed him softly. "Poor baby!"

He grinned. "Yep, you got me there."

"I'm sorry. I know my schedule has been crazy. Radiance and Javier are keeping me pretty busy. I'm also working with lawyers, agents, directors—you name it—for your upcoming movie. Woo! It's more than I can handle. I barely have time to paint. I'll tell you what—I can make time for you now, if you want." She straddled herself on top of him and smoothed his black hair with her hands.

"Sounds good to me. I'm beginning to feel better already. I know you have stepped into new territories and are in demand, but you have to promise to come to my studio," he said as his voice faded.

"I can't wait to see where this next season in our lives will take us," she said, kissing him all over. "I'll get back on board with my wifely duties tomorrow. It's four in the morning." She released his grip, rolled over to the other side of the bed, and pulled the covers over her head. "I have to be on the movie set by seven a.m."

Wellington was only half listening to Grace. In fact, he could see why he fell in love with her in the first place. She was always sexy and usually comfortably shy with him until he opened up her fiery and fierce appetite. This was no game. It was a treat that made her his everlasting love. Her body was athletic; her brown hair beautiful. Her eyes penetrating. Her wit quick, creative, and brilliant. The thought of her was forever new and exciting. The sweet smell of her sun-kissed body—oh, so rich and ripe—was intoxicating.

He could only see her mouth moving, her luscious lips just for him. He kissed everywhere he could find; then gently went inside her. *She is made for me, and we are one flesh*, he thought. Smiling and moving, he lifted himself up, never leaving her alone inside, first pulling off his shirt and then lifting her torso and taking her gown straight up and then onto the floor.

Grace thought, *Now he's started something, and he'd better look out!* She did not have to pretend to suddenly catch on to his new attitude. They gymnastically, passionately, and spiritually consummated, slowly and powerfully, the long-term matrimonial agreement that they loved to work on again and again, to get it just right. The Holmes' breath and bodies culminated in ecstasy, fulfilling their hunger, thirst, and desires to mold their love into one flesh.

CHAPTER

5

ℒAI Development

Grace arrived on set as the cast was taking a break during the filming of *The Wellington Holmes Story*. She noted the time difference between Switzerland where Monica lived and decided to call her.

"Hi, it's me. You got a moment?"

"Hey, Grace. You caught me just as I was getting ready to lie down for the night."

"Oh, I'm sorry. I won't keep you long. I have something I want to run past you. It's good to hear your voice."

"Yours too. Is all well with Wellington?"

"He's feeling better. I'm trying to get him to stick with Dr. Patel's orders. That is a priority. I'm on the movie set of his life story, waiting for the next scene, so I have a few minutes to talk. I left him at home and hope he will stick to his morning routine."

"How's the filming going?" asked Monica.

"It's just beginning, but so far, it's really good."

"You have something to ask me?"

"Yes. Girl, I had this idea that came to me in a dream—this time a crystal-clear dream. I believe God dropped it deep into my spirit because when I woke up, I could see it and hear it, and now I want to do it! You were in the dream as well."

"Really? You always talk about your dreams and how they have meaning."

"Well, listen to this one." Grace relayed the dream to Monica.

"Wow! Liquid Art Intelligence."

"I call it "LAI" for short," Grace interjected.

"That is revolutionary, and needed in the art world to stop these criminals from getting over on artists. Perhaps something like that could have saved Daniel's life."

"Yes. It might have. I'm calling to ask for your help with the research and development for something of this nature."

"I would love to help you develop this. It sounds like a great challenge, as well as an opportunity. What makes it exciting is the thought of supporting the art community. I know a top-notch chemical researcher we could bring on board," Monica said.

"I want to keep some of the talent within the Artist Wife Organization. I'm considering two of the artists' wives to participate in developing this innovative product."

"Who do you have in mind?" Monica asked.

"Tracey and Georgie from Upstate New York. You know they are brilliant chemical and structural engineers. I have an additional question. I wonder if we should develop this in Switzerland rather than in the United States. I know international laws are different, and they are subject to limited examination when registering intellectual property."

"I'll check that out," Monica said. "I have legal contacts who can advise me on that matter. This sounds like something on the cutting edge that will sweep the art world. I'll start on it first thing tomorrow."

"We have to make sure all parties involved sign confidentiality agreements before we get started. I wouldn't want this to leak out too soon," Grace insisted.

"Girl, you got me all worked up. I hope I can sleep tonight. You are on to something awesome."

"Correction—*we* are on to something awesome! I also reminded Wellington about the Swiss network interview next month. He's excited. I look forward to seeing you in a couple of weeks at our first West Coast Artist Wife Summit in Los Angeles. I can't wait to meet the speaker you selected."

"You won't be disappointed. Hopefully, I will have something to report on the development of the LAI when I see you. Tell Wellington hello."

"I will. Until then, take care," replied Grace.

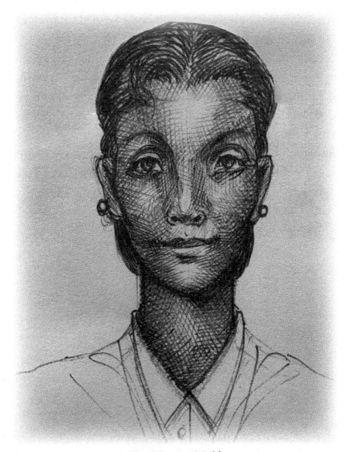
Dr. Monica Wolf

CHAPTER 6

Artist Wife Summit

Back in the day, a small group of women in New York City's Greenwich Village supported their husbands and significant others in their artistic careers. With Grace at the helm and Monica supporting, they had formed a quaint close-knit group that evolved into the Artist Wife Organization (AWO). Monica's husband, Daniel Wolf, was an exceptionally gifted artist who died in an unfortunate car accident. Dr. Monica Wolf, an epidemiologist specializing in autoimmune diseases at the CDC, moved to Switzerland after her husband's death for a special research assignment, but she remained loyal to the Artist Wife Organization. The organization was created as an outlet for wives to share their thoughts and experiences.

The organization quickly grew as an online chat forum for artists' wives of various artistic expressions.

Now, ten years later, the Artist Wife Organization was set to host their first national summit in Los Angeles at the Ritz-Carlton Marina del Rey. The guest speaker, Dr. Genevieve Snow, wife of the famous New York trumpeter, Tiger Snow, was the Phenomenal Woman of the Year. Grace's New York friend, Ellona Robie, and Grace's mother, Ruth Green, who lived in Santa Barbara, California, accompanied Grace to the premiere.

On the night of the event, Grace wore a black-and-white polka dot shirt dress by Coco Chanel, with a black leather belt that emphasized her modest twenty-four-inch waist. She accentuated her dress with Jimmy Choo classic black-and-white pumps, and pearl earrings.

As she paced the floor, awaiting the guest speaker's arrival, Monica appeared the ever cool and calm one. She was outfitted in a black-and-white pantsuit with heels to match. She was at ease as she jotted down last-minute notes. Ellona and Ruth sat quietly nearby, watching Grace sip from her alkaline water.

"Thanks, Monica, for making the travel arrangements for Dr. Snow to be our inaugural keynote speaker." The slight tremor in Grace's voice was evident.

"Girl, you are tense and jumpy. You need to relax. Dr. Snow will be awesome. She's spearheaded many women's forums in her day. The event will go smoothly. She will speak for twenty-five minutes and then open the floor for discussion."

"Do I look OK?" Grace asked. She fumbled with her silky brown hair; it fell in a precision cut just above her shoulders.

"You look great."

I should have let my hair grow long like yours. My hair grows too fast, and I don't like the color. Do you?"

"It goes well with your skin tone."

Grace dabbed the perspiration streaming from her forehead. "Did you see the huge crowd out there?"

"Don't focus on the crowd. Have you forgotten how natural you are when you speak to a group? Girl, please! Process your emotions! Obviously, God stretched you for this purpose. Your vision for the

Artist Wife Women On A Mission meet-up is perfect. You aren't afraid to take a risk to reach your greatness, and I commend you for that. It's almost showtime. Don't let fear grip you now," Monica exhorted her.

"It's still nerve-wracking. I scarcely know why God chose me to lead, but I did ask Him for courage to do what He's challenged me to do. It's just so big, and I want everything to go smoothly."

"It will if you calm yourself. Give yourself some credit, girl. So much has changed under your leadership. This organization already has had a far-reaching impact on many women. I heard someone—I can't remember who—speak about expansion. You better get ready, girl, because this is about to blow up."

"I hear you loud and clear. This is the season to help other artists' wives to address heartfelt issues. We can support, release tension, share ideas, and—hopefully—heal women as they figure out this Artist Wife lifestyle." Grace wiped her sweaty hands on a tissue. "I get it. I hear all the time from ladies who work in the corporate world. They talk about how different it is to be married to a creative individual. It's a way of life to which they have to adapt—we know that all too well."

"As a doctor, I can relate," Monica said. "When I married Daniel, it was a huge adjustment. The thing I loved and learned about art is that it heals, and we are blessed to be a part of this fascinating world. Surely, God is the greatest artist. Now, to understand artists is another issue. They think on the right side of the brain, and Lord knows that's not always easy to understand."

They laughed heartily.

"All I know is that as wives or partners, support is necessary, no matter what career each person has," Grace said. "I know that God is pushing me to step out on this venture, but I'm still unsure if I will say or do the right thing." She shrugged.

"I understand." Monica gave her a reassuring touch on her shoulder. "He will guide you. I have faith in you. As a leader you'll knock this out of the park."

"Thanks for the encouragement, sis." Grace gave her a big hug.

Dr. Genevieve Snow was escorted into the Green Room by Marcella, Grace's assistant who said, "Dr. Snow, I want you to meet Grace Holmes, the Artist Wife," she gestured towards Grace.

"So nice to meet you. I'm so happy you are here." Grace shook Dr. Snow's hand observing her tall, model-like stature and butterscotch complexion. She was in her early forties and wore an exquisite purple African gown with gold interwoven stitches and a matching head wrap.

"I'm so excited to be here. I read all about your organization and have been following you on Facebook and Instagram. You are surely women on a mission." She smiled, displaying deep dimples in both cheeks and a set of gorgeous white teeth.

"Would you care for some water?" Grace asked.

"Yes, please."

The meeting room was filled with a diverse group of women. Ellona, Ruth, Tracey, and Georgie sat in the front row next to a few art patrons.

"Ladies, let's make this happen!" Grace said to Monica and Dr. Snow as they strutted out of the Green Room.

Grace welcomed the crowd and was greeted by thunderous applause and a crowd roar that lasted a few minutes. After she quieted them, she spoke.

"Thank you for coming. Over ten years ago, with the help of Dr. Monica Wolf, we started a small chapter of the Artist Wife Organization in New York, and today, we are pleased to announce a new chapter on the West Coast in Los Angeles." She beamed and received roaring applause again.

"It takes courage, it takes strength, but most of all, it takes the love within each of you who support your loved one's visions to give us purpose. We all have individual lives, but sometimes that can slip away when you focus solely on your family. Sometimes, we forget that there is something that God has for us too. It is our goal to support creative loving relationships through healthy dialogue. We hope you will be transparent and share your experiences to help others. The purpose of the AWO is to strengthen each other as we build strong foundations for our families. I would like to share my beginnings as an artist's wife.

"My story—I started college as a quiet and extremely sheltered girl who desired to pursue a dream to become an artist. In my pursuit, I was clueless that I would fall in love so quickly or that I would marry an artist—that was not part of my plan. Once married, my husband shared with me that he never thought he would marry an artist either. Oh, well."

The crowd laughed.

"There is no perfect couple. But when love calls, you recognize it. So, ladies, do not ignore it. I was young when I got married. My husband at the time was an art professor and a budding artist whose career took off quickly. As an artist's wife, I found myself in unknown territory and up against some immoral characters in the art world. But God, our Father and deliverer, brought us through a difficult time in our marriage and in our careers. It was the beginning of a steep learning curve that made me strong, and for that, I am grateful. There is more to the story, but that is for another day. Ladies, there is no playbook for an artist's wife. Each situation is different. My motto is, 'It's a relationship you wouldn't understand'. Through our journey together, Dr. Monica and I have gained knowledge and significant experience as artists' wives. It is our desire to help you pave a healthy and joyful path for you and your family. That is the foundation on which this organization was created. We recently added a new initiative to shadow young artists. We plan on making our conferences a healthy space where we can talk, trust, support, one another, establish new business networks, and gain new friendships. We have created a Code of Conduct so that people listen and respect one other. It is OK to shed a tear and, of course, to laugh, which is the greatest healer. Most of all, we will find ways to have fun. So, without further ado, let me introduce my sister friend, and my colleague, Dr. Monica Wolf, who will introduce our guest speaker. Please put your hands together and welcome Dr. Monica Wolf."

Monica approached the microphone and received a hug from Grace.

"Thank you. Don't you all look lovely. Please join me in giving Grace a big hand for organizing this summit. What a woman of courage! I believe some of you may be familiar with our speaker today, Dr. Genevieve Snow, who recently received the Phenomenal Woman of the Year award. What an accomplishment. You can read about her achievements in your program. Today, she will talk to us about "Women On a Mission". We also want to hear from you after she finishes and opens the floor for comments. Please put your hands together and help me welcome Dr. Genevieve Snow. Dr. Snow approached the microphone and gave Monica nod of thanks.

"Thank you. I am honored to be here today. Thank you, Grace and Monica, for your gracious invitation. I am an artist's wife of fifteen years, so I will do my best to speak from my experiences. It is a joy and a daunting experience to be an artist's wife. To be a wife, period, for that matter, is a challenge unto itself. There is so much peace to be found when you embrace and learn to live with a creative genius. The goal is to listen and to be willing to provide support. That is your mission! You do that by being selfless and keeping your heart open. It takes two. I did not say it was an easy task. It is not. Love is the key. As women, we always want to vent, right? We cannot help it. God knows that because he made us. That is why it's important to form alliances with women like AWO. This crowd represents artists, artists' wives, companions, and even family members who support artists. It is time we put some issues of the heart on the table. They can be good or bad or indifferent, but the goal is to find answers, give encouragement, heal, and maybe even retool some things. It is important to know there is hope; to know that no relationship or marriage is perfect. It takes a willingness to agree to disagree and sometimes even walk away and cool off. Forgiveness is a major key in relationships of all kinds. I am reminded of the late, great Dr. Maya Angelou's book *Wouldn't Take Nothing for My Journey Now*.

She said, 'The woman warrior who is armed with wit and courage will be among the first to celebrate victory.' Women get ready for your mission!"

The ladies cheered and roared, stomped their feet, and clapped thunderously. By the time Dr. Snow finished, every lady in the room was on her feet with tears in her eyes. Dr. Snow opened the floor for questions; after she finished, she exited the stage to still more applause.

Grace stood at the podium and quieted the crowd. "Thank you, Dr. Snow, for your words of encouragement, insight, wisdom, and the dynamic, heartfelt message you gave today. As we embark on this new path, this new season and journey of expansion, let us remember to value our lives, dare to stretch out into the world of possibilities, dare to stand up, dare to speak up, and dare to dream. As artists' wives and/or companions, we pledge to love and think about our behavior. In addition, we will help other young women to become the best artists' wives possible. We want to create a new millennial network of artists' wives who will see a way through their issues and find their purposes inside themselves and outside their partners. There is a table at the back of the room for you to sign up for groups. We are planning future events and will keep you informed through our website and social media. This information is also in your program. We hope you have enjoyed yourselves. Thank you for coming. We look forward to seeing you at our next event. Please hug a couple of sisters before you leave. Thank you!"

Everyone mingled and headed to the tables for sign-ups, while Grace and Monica shared a confident look of approval.

"I want to meet with you, Tracey, and Georgie before I return to Switzerland to give you a rundown on my research on the new tool. You will be pleasantly surprised to know there is no tool out there like yours, and that is why we need to jump on this immediately. As the saying goes, if you think it, somebody else has thought it too," Monica said.

"I know that's right. I gave the girls a little background on it already. They are prepared to meet at any time."

"My plane doesn't leave until tomorrow afternoon. How about dinner this evening?"

"I can make reservations at Cast & Plow in the marina around six. I'll text you the address," Grace said.

"Sounds good."

"I'll let Tracey and Georgie know. I can't wait until you get a place in New York; then we will be closer," Grace smiled.

"It will be like old times. I hope to make that happen within the next couple of months. I will keep my place in Switzerland and work from both locations. Great job today, Grace."

"You too. I thank God for you. I could not do it without you."

They hugged before rejoining the others in the lobby.

CHAPTER

7

Meeting of the Minds

On Wednesday Grace sat with Dr. Monica Wolf, Tracey Vinson, and Georgie Houston on the patio of Cast & Plow in Marina del Rey, enjoying the evening breeze and the sounds of ocean waves crashing against the huge rocks. This was a perfect setting for their first real meeting to talk about a tool that could change the landscape of the criminal art world.

"Ladies, I hardly slept last night in anticipation of working with you on this project. Let's decide what we want to eat, and then we can talk. By the way, dinner is on me," Grace said, as the waitress took their orders. "Since Monica is in the country, I thought it would be a good time for the four of us to get together and see what each of us has to report on the Liquid Art Intelligence tool. Knowledge of how to develop something like this is way out of my league, so I'm leaning on you." Grace sipped her tea.

"First, let me express my sincere gratitude for being considered part of this project," Monica said. "I owe this to my dear husband, whose death was senseless. It is a true honor to put our collective minds together to develop this tool. There is nothing on the market like this. We are truly entering uncharted territory. For so long, art thieves have been stealing our work and making us look like fools. It is high time that we took steps to turn this situation around."

"I spoke with Tracey and Georgie and told them a little about the project," Grace said. "Now, ladies, we want to hear your feedback."

Tracey spoke first. "We have a few questions for you."

"Go ahead," Grace said.

"Is this going to be used to authenticate the artist's signature on the painting?"

"No. The signature has no significance. This will be something liquid, like an atomizer spray applied to the back of paintings to track the art's originality. The spray will be harmless to the painting itself. The purpose is to make it difficult for thieves to steal valuable original paintings and artifacts."

"Is it for museum use only?" Tracey asked.

"It is for museums and private owners."

"Then we probably are on the right track." Tracey nodded to Georgie.

"We researched and found a way to track stolen assets by using an invisible ink—a tan organic compound that can be detectable under a certain light spectrum to prove the authenticity or the value of its originality," Georgie said.

"That's incredible." Grace smiled.

"Think of it as a band similar to what is on twenty-dollar bills or other money to authenticate its value," Georgie added.

"That sounds like a method we should test," Monica chimed in.

"Also, you need to be aware that there are dark web places where criminals speak to each other. They are known as underground forums," Georgie said.

"How do we avoid them?" Grace inquired.

"We would use digital tracking, like forensics. This could be a 3D resin printer, like the stereolithography 3D printer, which is designed in a CAD program for the printer. But we will test different methods to see which one proves the best for what you are trying to accomplish," Tracey summed up.

Grace frowned. "Sounds so techie. I know that God placed you on my mind as the women who could help with this development, so I feel confident in what you're telling us. On that note, I think I am going to add you two to my Angels in Disguise team." Grace smiled.

"That's a high honor—to be considered an aid who comes to your rescue." Tracey smiled. "And there's more."

"Lord, my head is already spinning, but don't let me stop you now. I am loving this ingenuity," Grace said.

"Other thoughts are how to control the tracking integrity of the compound through our registration process of the art and keeping our trade secret or patent intact. It depends on what is decided. We will have art curators and law enforcement evaluate our product and our process before we go to market. We want to identify a supplier who is compliant and certified with the International Organization for Standardization. There are worldwide proprietary, industrial, and commercial standards to follow that ensure the quality, safety, and efficiency of products, services, and systems, such as quality management, environmental management, information security, management systems, and social responsibility, to name a few. We know this is high-level technical talk for you but be assured that we will simplify this language so you can understand each step of the process."

"I appreciate that, ladies. I have enough in my world to think about."

"Grace, I checked with attorneys, and they suggested there is an advantage to registering the tool in Switzerland. They also will look into a regulatory bureau and an international consortium to handle the regulation of the product associated with law enforcement," Monica added.

"Ladies, I'm overwhelmed. It is obvious that you covered all areas. Going forward, we will continue our discussions on this matter, which will include how we will handle costs and expenses. I appreciate you so much. Now, let's toast to the development and success of this LAI product." Grace raised her glass, and they all joined her. "We agree this tool will be a creative breakthrough and a light in a dark place that will restore relationship integrity in the art world."

"Hear, hear!" they said in unison.

"Now let's eat before our food gets cold," Grace said. She felt a deep sense of contentment, satisfaction, and gratitude.

CHAPTER 8

Artist Studio Party

Owema-A's Gallery in the affluent New York City SoHo community featured four elite artists from across the globe. It was Grace's first show since her new abstract collection, titled *Grace Overflow*, made national headlines. Max Shelton, an African American art representative introduced by Ty Hamilton and with whom Grace signed an artist contract, pulled major strings to include her in this elite show. Wellington, however, the featured artist of the show, did not commit to agency representation.

When they arrived, the atmosphere was electric, filled with the loud chatter of art collectors, politicians, businessmen and businesswomen, professional models, and athletes. All eyes were on Salvador Franco from Sardinia, inarguably one of the greatest portrait painters in Italy. Smooth jazz played softly in the background, while a growing crowd watched him paint a beautiful Japanese woman. Her silky black hair, pulled back in a long ponytail, reached all the way to her waist. She had high cheekbones and lovely eyes. She wore a long beige silk dress with burgundy knee-high boots, visible by her crossed legs. Grace learned later that the lady was Kiko Yamamoto, an international model.

A distinguished, well-groomed man with a cane stood at the edge of the crowd with a sparkle in his eye. Grace's straight brown hair flipped at her shoulders and swung freely as she stepped with poise. She wore a glittery silver top with black straight-leg pants that stopped above the ankle to show off her black Coco Chanel pumps. Wellington, walking alongside her, wore a white silk shirt and a dark blue Armani suit. As they passed by, Salvador's eyes followed Grace to the extent that she blushed and felt vulnerable, as if his eyes had truly studied her entire body and her every move. Later, during the show, she observed Salvador intently studying her full red lips. She quickly looked away. Grace mingled with many guests and all the artists during the show—except Salvador.

He approached her silently without her noticing. He was a bronzed-skin Italian with brown eyes and a distinct chiseled jawline. He wore white jeans and a perfectly pressed black shirt, opened enough to reveal his hairy chest. One might say he was a *bell uomo*—handsome man. When he spoke in his lyrical falsetto, it was almost impossible for Grace to make out his words. He said that he wanted to paint her portrait. Grace heard him but did not respond. They exchanged business cards, and she excused herself from his compelling presence to chat with others. Kiko's face displayed disdain during Grace and Salvador's interaction. Wellington didn't notice at all. Grace didn't know what to make of the experience.

Salvador

Kiko

SEASON 2
Family Does Matter

CHAPTER 9

Swiss Interview

As Grace explained to Mia Keller, TV analyst from SRF 1 in Bern, Switzerland, "The power of trust and transparency can change and heighten a relationship. When Wellington and I got married, we agreed that trust and transparency were the most important elements in our relationship. Along the way, we lost it, but we reconciled, and our relationship was restored. God is our burden bearer."

"Wellington, it's so good to have you and your wife, Grace, join us for this interview before the release of the new movie about your life," Mia Keller said. "I believe this is the first interview for you in several years."

Wellington nodded. "Yes. I had many offers, but the timing wasn't right. Thank you for inviting us to Switzerland and including us in this interview with Dr. Monica Wolf. I truly owe the Swiss people so much for helping me after my crisis. Dr. Monica talked me into this one."

"I'm glad she did," Keller told him. "You are in great demand, and I consider it an honor to be one of the first to get an interview with you. I understand that several production companies were vying for the right to the movie deal."

Wellington nodded again. "Yes. It's been so many years since the plane crash. I thank God for Dr. Monica's staff and for saving me. I also thank Dr. Monica and her team of doctors who rescued me and skillfully put me back together. God was watching over me, for sure. There was prayer and readjustments. My wife, Grace, went through a lot in those days without me, especially since she was pregnant at the time of the crash. The stress of it all caused her to lose our first child. She managed to stay strong, and she worked through her pain with the help of our families, counseling, and good friends. Once the time was right for her, she returned to our academy for the arts to pick up where we left off, and she worked relentlessly to keep the Wellington Holmes Art Academy alive. What a woman!"

"That is not an easy undertaking for any woman," Keller said.

Wellington couldn't hide a slight grimace. "I can't imagine what I put her through. On my end, my recovery was not easy. There were many days of lying in the bed, helpless, with no knowledge of who I was. I had anxiety, and depression tried to win. My body was pretty torn up, and I didn't know if I was going to live. One day while lying there in bed, I had an overwhelming feeling to fight for my life because God had more for me to do. I cannot explain it, but it was a *knowing* deep within me that He was not finished with me yet. "As I got stronger each day from the therapy that Dr. Monica suggested, my memory began to return. That's when I started returning to a normal life. Several biblical characters had some form of anxiety. They may not have called it *anxiety* back then, but King David was one of them. He spoke in the Psalms on several occasions of being troubled and in deep despair. He was very honest about it. David used words like *downcast, brokenhearted,* and *troubled.* Here was a godly man of faith who struggled and battled through dark times of hopelessness and depression. I couldn't remember my own wife and son. My Bible reading gave me hope during my time of recovery, that I was not alone and that it was part of the human condition."

Keller turned toward Grace. "Grace, what were your feelings when you heard that Wellington's plane went down?"

"I went into pure shock. It was a difficult time in my life. Nobody likes officers in uniforms showing up at their door early in the morning. It means only one dreadful thing. I blamed myself for all that went wrong. When we were first married, we agreed we would be transparent in our relationship. All hell broke loose the night before his accident, and he stormed out of our hotel room in anger. The next morning, when the officers appeared at my door and told me the news, I was a wreck. The following days were a complete blur. I lost our child and my husband, and I felt like I was losing my damn mind! I don't want to go into too much reflection because it will be revealed in the upcoming movie. I will say this, though: after many days of grief, I started practicing self-compassion and treated myself with kindness. Hope whispered to me and put things into perspective for me to keep going. I made the most of a bad situation. Instead of drawing negative conclusions or thoughts about my life, I made myself useful. With God's help, I pulled myself up and went to work at the Wellington Holmes Art Academy to uphold Wellington's legacy."

Keller smiled softly at Grace. "That is a beautiful story."

"There is more," Grace said. "We were dealing with an individual who already had murdered people; he attacked my personal integrity, and he tried to take my husband's life. There were losses, disappointments, and adjustments I had to make without Wellington. What this person did to my family was an irredeemable act, which will be revealed in the movie. As I said, I don't want to give all the details before our viewers see it." Grace smiled. "We are grateful that we have an opportunity to share our drama and our love story. It is a story of redemption and restoration."

"There was a painting involved somewhere in this story that caused some confusion—am I right?"

Grace was sensitive to questions about the infamous painting that started all the trouble. She hesitated before she answered. "Yes, this was a major part of a test I failed. A painting was created for a spring show at the Johansson Gallery in Switzerland. That is all I can say about it right now. That part will be revealed in the movie." She tried not to show any sign of sadness.

Keller leaned forward. "Grace, if I may ask one more question—what was it about the painting that caught the attention of the Johansson Gallery?"

Grace knew Keller was still digging, so she provided a quick on-the-spot answer. "Niklas and Laine Johansson loved Wellington's work and loved the hidden angel in the abstract. It was different from anything they had seen in Wellington's previous works. As I said, you will learn more when the movie is released in theaters." She managed a smile.

"We can hardly wait for this thriller," Keller said. "Grace, I want to switch the conversation to the product you recently developed for art security. I understand it will revolutionize the art world."

"So much has happened I don't know where to begin. The Liquid Art Intelligence, known as LAI, will help track original paintings once they leave the owners' hands. The development of this product is in its infancy. We are moving along with it, and it's being reviewed by experts as we speak. The goal now is to get qualified feedback and to find out the type of changes that are necessary to make it a highly accurate tool to deter theft."

"That is exciting," Keller said. "I cannot wait until it is released." She shifted her attention once again. "Now, to Dr. Monica Wolf—I want to ask you some questions about Wellington. How did you manage, day by day, to stay confident about his recovery and, at the same time, stay out of harm's way from the police or from anyone finding out he was alive? Were you ever in fear they would locate him?"

"Yes, it was scary," Monica admitted. "All I could do is trust God. Believe me—I had many sleepless nights, but as Grace said, we want to hold the suspense until the movie is released."

"Monica, did you fear being indicted for concealing Wellington?" Keller asked.

"I did! Fear tried to dominate me daily, but I restrained it. I had nightmares of all kinds that someone would discover that Wellington was alive. My dreams ranged from threats to people chasing me and even my death. I woke up many nights in a panic and had to seek God in prayer. I also got some therapy for my sleep disorder. I questioned whether I had made the right decision. Like Grace, I came to grips with seeking justice for all involved. We were all determined to get a bad thug off the streets."

"We?" Keller asked.

"Yes. Grace calls us her Angels in Disguise—her AID. Grace was resilient and the twenty-first century shero in this story. Through all her losses, being blackmailed, and handling thugs, she had no other choice but to become a warrior. She fought for her husband's life, his school, and his legacy. Once I told her that Wellington was alive, she also had to find strength to be patient until his return to his normal life."

"What a powerful story," Keller said. "I can see why the production companies fought for the movie rights to this story."

Wellington shifted in his chair and then spoke up. "Several studios approached us for the rights, but we gave Lionsgate Entertainment the green light to produce it."

"It's quite an intriguing story," Monica said. "It changed all of our lives and drew all of us closer to God. We pray that this story will help other artists and artists' wives as they continue to support one other."

"That's a blessing," Keller said. "What is the title of the movie, Wellington, and what can the audience expect?"

"The title is *The Wellington Holmes Story*. All of it was possible because of God's grace. My hope is that the story is told from a purely realistic standpoint and not so much a commercial kind of Hollywood fluff, if you know what I mean."

"I do understand," Keller said. "I would like to jump to another subject right now. Dr. Wolf, congratulations on the award for the development of an amazing vaccine that will save many lives. Your work in infectious diseases is groundbreaking. You are being recognized as a medical innovator and are making waves in the medical community, refining technologies to treat autoimmune diseases."

"It is an honor," Monica said. "As a doctor, I developed a vaccine for women and children. It was determined that bacteria in the Pacific Ocean was making people ill, which apparently started with an oil spill some years ago. Thousands died as a result. We have designed a public awareness campaign so that people will know about it. We've been working on this vaccine for several years. To find this cure is a true miracle. It helped that we were able to get some private investors to move it forward."

"Nice. Is there a number that people can call to find out more information?"

"Yes, they can go to the website shown at the bottom of the screen or call the number as well. Also, if you would like to donate to the cause, you can also call that same number. We appreciate your help."

"Can you share one example where you had success with the vaccine?" Keller asked.

Dr. Wolf nodded. "Yes. As a matter of fact, Wellington and Grace's son, Javier, was diagnosed at an early age with the Salton Sea disease. The vaccine saved his life. He is a young man now, and the vaccine made a significant change in his health. It is a miracle, and we thank God for the blessing. Unfortunately, his biological mother's condition was advanced, and after a short period in hospice, she passed away."

"I am sorry to hear that. Well, thank you all. Any last plug you want to add? Anyone?"

"I would like to give a big shout-out to my fans," Wellington said, "to Ty Hamilton and his investors for their donation to the Wellington Holmes Art Academy, which will pave the way for the next generation of artists."

Grace then added, "Dr. Maya Angelou, one of my favorite writers, said in her book, *Letter to My Daughter*, 'Be certain that you do not die without having done something wonderful for humanity.' That is my motive in creating LAI as a tool to reduce crime and danger in the fine arts world."

"I believe that it will," Keller said, "Thank you all again for coming. Oh yeah, Grace—that good ol' Swiss dark chocolate you asked about: it's waiting for you after this interview. Folks, there you have it—our guests, Grace Holmes, a phenomenal artist who designed a security tool for the art community, and her husband, artist Wellington Holmes, whose story is in preproduction at Lionsgate Studios, and Dr. Monica Wolf, a research scientist at the Centers for Disease Control, who developed a vaccine for mothers and children. Thank you for joining us to celebrate the incredible talent of these trendsetters. I'm Mia Keller, reporting to you from SRF 1 in Bern, Switzerland. Please join us again. Goodnight."

CHAPTER

10

The Wellington Holmes Story

Grace arrived at the Church of St. John the Divine on Amsterdam Avenue in Manhattan, where the filming of *The Wellington Holmes Story* was in high production.

"He killed my husband and that was enough for me to seek revenge," the actress playing Grace said, turning to the camera in a rage. "He was all that I had. He was my man, my husband, my hero. It brought out a rage in me that I could not silence."

"Cut," the director said. "Let's take thirty."

Grace wiped her brow as she watched the scene from the sidelines. The young lady playing her role was inspiring. Grace and Wellington never dreamed that a global television and film platform like Lionsgate Entertainment would approach them for a movie bio of Wellington Holmes.

In real life Wellington was dealing with anxiety attacks that had plagued him since his plane crash incident. The doctor said the best way to deal with the feelings was with rest and medication. While under distress in Switzerland, Wellington remembered reading the passage in Isaiah 30:15—"In quietness and trust shall be your strength." Reconnecting with Grace brought a spirit of ease back into his life and a reminder of her love for him. Now, Wellington knew that he had a future to look forward to, but for some reason, he felt irritable. He had a beautiful wife, two beautiful children, and a thriving career. Dr. Patel and Monica encouraged him to slow his schedule down. He found that was hard to do. With anxiety rising, he could not stand another moment of staying in the house. In his restlessness, and against Grace's advice, he made up his mind to go to the movie set.

Grace purposely had left him at home, knowing that the plane crash scene was being filmed. She was unaware that Wellington had arrived on the set. The scene showed when Azul and Wellington were talking at the airport and Wellington sensed something was wrong. Wellington watched the filming from the sidelines as the plane descended and plunged into Lake Geneva in Switzerland. The fiery crash was a reenactment of Azul's secret plan to kill him. After witnessing that, the real Wellington walked away in a hurry. Grace turned and noticed him and ran after him.

"I told you not to come today. You knew they were filming that scene," she fussed.

"I just had to see it for myself. I didn't mean to upset you." His voice was soft now and different. Nothing like Grace was accustomed to.

"You are the one upset. Look at you! Breathing heavily and holding your head. Are you OK?" She helped him to a nearby chair.

His skin tone had changed, and he held his head between his

knees. The pain started at his temples and ran down across the base of his neck. It hurt for him to sit up.

Grace recalled Wellington's increased restlessness and poor sleeping habits and knew something was off. She dialed Monica's number. *Come on, Monica, answer the telephone!* she thought. When she heard Monica's voice on the line, that did not change the fear in her voice. "Monica, hey. I'm here on the movie set with Wellington."

Monica instantly sensed something was wrong. "Calm down, Grace, and take a breath. Tell me what's going on."

"I told Wellington they were filming the plane crash scene today and that he shouldn't come. You know how stubborn he is. He showed up anyway. Now, he's devastated. He's complaining of dizziness and a headache. I happened to see him out of the corner of my eye, walking away and looking disturbed, and I ran after him. He was holding his head."

"Take a deep breath," Monica repeated.

"He's sitting with his head between his knees. I can't get a word out of him."

"I think I know what's happening. I don't want you to panic."

"Just tell me what to do," Grace said impatiently.

"Sometimes, seeing a replay of a traumatic event can cause stress. Let me ask you a few questions. Has he been sleeping well at night?"

"Intermittently. Why do you ask?"

"It is part of the beginning of the trauma. How long has it been since he had a full night's rest?"

"Probably a couple of weeks. He gets about three to four hours a night; then he's up and might lie back down, but he pops up in the morning, seemingly refreshed."

"That's not enough rest for him," Monica said. "Here's what I want you to do. Call 911 and get him to New York Presbyterian Hospital–Columbia. I will meet you there. Call me when you get there."

"I didn't expect him to come to the set today. He just showed up. There I go again, causing pain," Grace said.

"Grace, please! Just get him to the hospital. We will talk about that later. We need to examine him and do some tests. It's probably not as serious as you are making it, so stop worrying."

"OK. I'm sorry."

"I'm glad I'm here in New York for this conference."

"Me too. Thank God." Grace sighed.

"I know he will be fine. The doctors will confirm everything that is going on."

"OK," Grace said with tears in her eyes.

Monica dialed Dr. Patel's number. "This is Dr. Monica Wolf. May I speak to Dr. Patel?"

"He's out of the office. Can I have him call you?"

"Is there a way you can reach him?" Monica asked in a demanding tone. "It's rather urgent."

"Hold the line. I'll see what I can do, Dr. Wolf."

After a long pause, Dr. Patel came on the line. "Hey, Monica. My assistant told me it was urgent. What's going on?"

"Thanks for taking the call. I'm in New York for a conference. Grace Holmes just called me in a semi-panic. Wellington showed up on his movie set, and he's complaining of headaches. Something may have triggered and traumatized him."

"Thank God you are in New York. Where are you, and where is he?"

"I'm in a conference room. I told Grace to take him to New York Presbyterian Hospital–Columbia. I'm going to meet them there."

"Here's what I want you to do when you arrive," he said and then gave her instructions.

"Thank you, my friend. I am on it. I'll get back with you after I reach the hospital and will give you a report once I know what's going on."

"My assistant knows how to reach me. Keep me advised."

"Thanks. I appreciate it."

Monica hung up the telephone and dialed Grace. "I'm on my way. I also spoke with Dr. Patel."

"What did he say?" Grace asked.

"To have the hospital run specific tests. We knew this could happen at some point, considering the pressure Wellington's been under with his art exhibitions, teaching, and now seeing a reenactment of what happened to him. I'll be there in thirty minutes."

"It's my fault," Grace cried. "I should not have let him on the movie set at all."

"You mustn't let him see you break down, girl. He is going to be all right. Dr. Patel probably need to adjust his meds or something like that. I don't want you to think the worst. Pull yourself together. I'll be there soon."

"I'll do my best. Thank you," Grace said in between sniffles.

"Better yet, lead him in prayer," Dr Monica said.

Dr. Monica made a note to write in her journal later about Wellington's recurring headaches.

> *He hasn't been on the prazosin*, she thought. *Dr. Patel prescribed that for PTSD but that left him drowsy. Wellington thought he was fine and that he didn't need it any longer. It was a repeat of symptoms that he experienced after the crash—inability to sleep, frequent episodes of anxiety, and signs of depression.*

Monica arrived at the hospital around the same time as the ambulance. She touched Grace's arm as the ER staff unloaded Wellington and entered the hospital. Monica gave Grace a confident look, reminding her to "keep it together."

Grace nodded in return and blew a kiss to Wellington, who was under an oxygen mask.

"Lord, help!"—that was all Grace could say as she dialed her mom's number. Keenly aware of the presence of her fearful thoughts, she prayed them back.

∼

"Hey, Mom. I need your prayers."

"What's wrong?" Ruth asked, concerned by Grace's tone.

"We were on the movie set and something triggered in

Wellington's mind as he watched the crash scene. Monica and Dr. Patel believe he was traumatized. Dr. Blackwell, the physician at the hospital, is running tests to determine his medical condition. I haven't told you some of the things he has been experiencing lately," Grace said, feeling guilty.

"Take a breath, baby."

"Monica thinks they need to change his meds. Only thing I need you to do is pray. I'm believing God that he's going to be OK."

"My dear, what's next for you two? I understand everyone is pulling you from every side. That's what happens when your life blows up. Oh well, it won't do me any good to fuss now. I'll pray, and I can get on a plane if you need me."

"You are a stabilizing force in my life. I'm going to need your strength from right where you are," Grace affirmed.

"Where are Javier and Radiance?"

"Ellona is going to pick them up."

Ruth reminded Grace to rest it all in God's hands. "I love you baby." Grace forced a wry smile before hanging up.

~

After a few hours, Wellington opened his eyes and smiled. Grace and Monica sat quietly next to his bedside.

"Thanks for coming, Monica," Wellington said, trying to sit up.

"How are you feeling?" Monica asked. Grace adjusted his pillow.

"A little drowsy from the meds and exhausted from all the tests. God was trying to get my attention, but I guess I was too busy." He looked at Grace.

"It can happen," Dr. Blackwell said, entering the room and checking Wellington's pupils. "I want to share the results with you. The specific lab tests confirmed depression symptoms were not related to your prior condition."

"That's a good thing," Monica said.

Dr. Blackwell then explained, "Many central nervous system illnesses and injuries can lead to depression, such as head trauma, which you experienced in the crash years ago. The hospital also gave standard tests to rule out any other diagnoses—CT scans or MRI of the brain to rule out serious illness, such as a brain tumor. The ECG to diagnose any heart problems. The EEG to record electrical activity of the brain. Blood tests to check for medical conditions that might cause depressive symptoms." He smiled. "This occurrence was a mild setback, and it's treatable. Traumatic brain injury is serious, but with rest and obeying what your doctors say, you will be fine." He patted the end of Wellington's bed and left the room.

"I know God is one who heals," Wellington said. "I may have ongoing memory challenges, word-finding challenges, aphasia, even vertigo, but my challenges pales in comparison to those faced by the other survivors," Wellington said.

"He's right, Grace," Monica said. "In fact, many have not survived what Wellington's been through. When I look at his case from that perspective, there are a lot of reasons to be very hopeful about his hard data and the factual information about his new treatments."

Grace sighed. "That is comforting to hear."

"You know, the brain is plastic but elastic. It won't bounce back to where it was. We continue to evolve, and neuroplasticity works wonders. Once you returned to New York, your career took off again, and that pressure caused unwanted anxiety. You have been sustainable in your recovery. Some of your life memories were erased, but they came back! You defied the odds. That is why your life story is in high demand by the studios. In your six-month physical, Dr. Patel and I noticed your forward progress. Your PTSD nightmares have slowed. Your current challenge is due to sleep deprivation and not a backslide in brain injury recovery. The lack of sleep exacerbates brain injury symptoms. You need to get back to regular sleep patterns. You need at least eight hours, and you will see relief from this recent flare-up of brain injury. That is what the Dr. Patel ordered, right?" Monica smiled.

Wellington returned her smile. "I hear you. Grace has been on me about that. I plan to do better. That feeling on the set was scary, and I cannot have that happen again. I have a wife and two children who need me."

"And we have criminals to chase," Detective Ramos said, entering the room.

Everybody laughed.

"How's my guy?" Ramos asked.

"Hey, everybody's here. I must be important after all!" Wellington smiled.

"Man, you are valuable to us. I rushed over as soon as Grace called me. After all we've been through together, I feel like family. It sounded urgent, so I had to come to see about you. I overheard someone say you're going to be fine."

"I hope so," Wellington said. "I know I need to slow down."

"We need you, man, so listen to your doctors and to your wife." Detective Ramos chuckled.

"The season of rest has been ordered. Now I need help to get him to obey," Grace said with a grimace.

CHAPTER

11

Sibling Rivalry

"I'm ashamed of you," Radiance Holmes said to her brother, Javier.

"Why?" Javier asked unabashedly.

"Because you posted that story. It's fake news!"

He laughed. "Girl, you don't know what fake news is. You heard that from somebody."

"I watch CNN! I'm almost fifteen, and I'm more alert than you think. Just because you're older, you do *not* know everything!" she snapped.

"You got it wrong, Radiance. Writing is among the many talents I have. It goes right along with painting, dancing, and anything I want to do creatively. I am going to end up in Hollywood one day. You'll see."

"You are arrogant and disgusting," she said, pushing him away.

"I'm just confident. You're too young to understand the difference between arrogance and confidence. Do you know how long it took me to get to this point?"

"I don't care to know. I'm sure I've already heard it."

"I'm going to tell you anyway, you spoiled little brat. I was sheltered for most of my life. You were too young to remember how shy I was when I first came to live here with the family. I barely had a voice." He smiled. "I was small for my age and had low self-esteem. I had just lost my mother. I was in transition. The kids teased me because of my size and because I was African-Mexican. Then, after my mother died, it took years for me to come out of my shell. Anyway, kid, look at me now! I'm six feet tall, good looking, and all those zits are gone from my face." He smoothed his hands over his face. "In fact, girls chase me every day. I knew Dad and Grace loved me, but I had to learn to love myself. 'It's my season,'" he sang, smiling in her face. "Besides, what I posted isn't any different from everyone else. Trust me on this, lil sis. Just watch what happens after this post goes viral."

"OK, but if we get in trouble with Dad, you have to take the hit," Radiance said, pouting.

"What happens when we become famous, like Dad and Mom? Are you gonna take the credit and convince them it was your idea, like you usually do about everything? 'I'm the baby,'" he said, mocking her.

"Stop teasing me!" she cried. "I just hate that you made that video. Dad and Mom are going to kill us when they see it because I'm underage."

"Relax. You're stressing for nothing. They won't see it. Plus, there's no harm in the video. I'll take the blame, any way it goes. I can't help that I got swag. I think you are tripping and jealous. Besides, I had to outdo the others—I'm the best student in art school."

"Yes, you are," Radiance said reluctantly. "But you don't have to rub it in."

"I don't show off with the other students. Only with you because you are my sister, and I'm trying to teach you—"

"You don't need to teach me nothing!" she screamed. "I can stand on my own two feet."

"There you go again, getting defensive. I'm trying to help you. We could be a good team if you'd stop whining and acting like a baby."

"Dad favors you because you are the budding artist in the family!" she cried.

The front door opened, and Wellington walked into the room. "What's going on here? Radiance, why are you crying?"

"You and Mom never stop talking about how Javier excels." She ran to his side. "Everywhere I look in the academy, there are pictures of him and all his awards. You favor him more than me."

"That's not true, nor is it fair for you to say that, young lady," Wellington said. "Javier is much older than you are and is developing as an artist. He's nineteen and preparing for college. You know that your mother and I have taken trips with Javier to Howard University and Cooper Union and a few other art schools for admissions interviews. You should be proud of him, not fighting with him. We saw your talents at age three and we know that you also have artistic ability. You should not be so hard on Javier. He made a big adjustment when he came to live with us."

"Well, he's always in my space," she said.

"You have no *space*, young lady. This house is owned by me and your mother. You got that?"

"Yes, sir. He rubs me the wrong way." She stuck her lip out in a pout.

Wellington hugged her. "That's natural for brothers and sisters."

"See? There you go, soaking up the hugs," Javier said.

"You are just jealous!" She stuck her tongue out at him.

"Stop it, you two!" Wellington shouted. "We have something more important to concentrate on. You need to make up and stop all this foolishness. Your mother and I love both of you just the same. Right now, the big art contest next week is important, and we plan on winning it. But it's not going to happen if you two aren't a team and are not on the same page, working together. Remember that you are privileged to attend my academy for free. Sometimes, I think you both are ungrateful."

"Dad, I'm sorry," Javier apologized. "It's all my fault. We are grateful for what we have. I promise I won't act like this again."

Radiance stuck out her tongue at Javier again and moved closer to Wellington.

Javier lunged toward her.

"Dad, tell him to stop!" Radiance cried. She pushed Javier away. "He's beyond help."

Wellington shook his head. "I need to sit both of you down and teach you a lesson in humility. The creative gifts you have are more for others than for yourself," he explained. "I thought we taught you that. By the way, where is your mother?"

"She's on the movie set. She said she'll be home by six."

"Go get in the car," he urged them. "We have work to do."

They pushed and shoved each other on the way to the car, even though they loved each other deeply.

Radiance Holmes

Javier Holmes

CHAPTER

12

Radiance's World

At age fourteen, Radiance was very much like Grace. She was confident and imaginative; she read a lot and had only a handful of friends—but that changed on the day she met fifteen-year-old Makayla, the most popular girl in the school. To Radiance's surprise, she was invited to sit with Makayla's select group of friends. Makayla was a caramel-colored African-Mexican girl with sharp features. She had thick, bouncy, kinky hair; and a big, bubbling personality.

One day during lunch, Radiance noticed Makayla's tattoo and asked her about it.

"You like it?" Makayla displayed a small heart on the back of her left shoulder.

"It's simple and cute."

"My boyfriend's best friend, Ricardo, did it."

"You have a boyfriend? And your mom doesn't mind your having a tattoo?" Radiance asked.

"Not really. I'm an only child. As long as my grades are good, she says yes to a lot of things I ask."

"I wish my mom and dad were lenient. They are very protective."

"I wouldn't know," Makayla replied matter-of-factly. "My mom trusts me to do the right thing. Teenagers need to have fun too. As long as I behave responsibly, then there's no problem."

"Yes, I guess," Radiance replied.

"I plan on getting another tattoo soon. Would you like to come with me?" Makayla asked.

"I would love to, but I don't know. I need to check my mom's schedule first. If it is cool, I'll arrange to go home with you after school," Radiance said, delighted by the invitation.

"Girl, I pity all y'all who have to check in."

"It's not a problem. I'm young, and my parents have standards they expect me to keep."

"That's cool, I guess. Anyway, Tommy is here," Makayla said, pointing at the waiting motorcycle.

A guy in a black leather jacket, with short dreads sticking out from underneath his helmet, waved at her.

"I got to go!" She ran toward him.

Radiance envisioned that kind of fun and freedom, but she knew she would probably have to wait a few more years. Getting a tattoo lingered as a far-fetched thought. *Maybe I could get one in an area where mom wouldn't notice*, she thought.

After school on Thursday, Radiance and Makayla headed to Ricardo's studio for the tattoo appointment.

As they entered the garage of Ricardo's family home, which served as his studio, Makayla said to him, "This is my friend Radiance."

"Hey," Radiance said shyly.

His light-scented cologne filled the air and tickled her nostrils.

He nodded and continued to eye her before he began creating Makayla's design.

Radiance noticed his smooth skin and the ponytail that fell at the nape of his neck. She saw the colorful tattoos that covered his forearms.

As he drew Makayla's tattoo, the pain was visible on her face. Ricardo turned to Radiance and asked, "Are you next?"

Radiance shook her head. "I'm not ready today, but I'll think about it."

After they left, Radiance asked Makayla about Ricardo. "He's got a nice studio. How old is he?"

"Sixteen."

"Where did you meet him?"

"He was painting tattoos at one of Tommy's parties. He's been accepted at Juilliard."

"Wow. That's an honor. I don't think I've seen him before. But he couldn't have been accepted based on painting tattoos."

"Girl, of course not. That's his passion on the side. He's an exceptional dancer and choreographer. His live performance at a recent party put everyone there in a popular network video. It was so cool! You should come to a party."

"That *is* impressive, and he's sort of cute. I wish I could go to some parties, but I know I can't. I do want a tattoo, but my mother would *not* approve, and my older brother, Javier, would surely tell on me."

"Girl, everybody has them. Think about it. If you change your mind, I'll set it up for you."

Radiance nodded and let the thought linger.

Over the next few weeks, Radiance noticed Tommy and Ricardo sitting on their motorcycles at the curb after school. Makayla and Tommy would ride away, leaving Ricardo, in his black leather jacket, to sit and stare at Radiance. Each time she walked away, and he would ride off—but today was different.

He started his motorcycle and sped up behind her. "Want a ride home?" he asked as he slowed his bike.

"No, I can walk."

"Have you ever been on a motorcycle?"

"No." She continued to walk and avoid eye contact.

"Then you don't know how exciting it can be. I guarantee you will like it. We can take a ride, and I'll bring you right back to school after a ride around the block or two."

"No, I don't think so," she said, walking faster.

"Oh, come on. It won't hurt you. It will be fun—you'll see." He pulled in front of her and stepped off the bike.

His six-foot-one frame towered over her, and she noticed the deep dimple in his left cheek when he smiled.

"I barely know you. What makes you think I'm that easy that I'll just say yes, just because all the other girls probably do?"

"You don't know me either, but you're judging me."

"Well, is it true?"

"I'm not telling you." He smiled. "But I will say this. I know you're going to a fine school and got that privilege thing going on, so if you said no to an outsider, I would understand."

"I know you're friends with Makayla and her boyfriend, but maybe you could tell me a little something about yourself to at least make me comfortable about riding with you."

"What do you want to know? OK. Let me start with this—we have something in common."

"What?"

"I'm an artist too. I dabble in a few art forms. I have a little history."

"Yes, I heard. Makayla told me you were accepted to Juilliard. That is no little dabbling affair."

"Yes, that's true. I'm pretty excited about it, but I don't have a big head about it. What I really love to do on the side is create tattoos. It's a passion! So, don't look down on me like I'm so different than you because you see me hanging around the school on my motorcycle.

The only difference in our art forms is I like to create paintings on skin rather than on paper. That's how I look at it."

"I'm not looking down at you. I just want to know more about you."

"Well, are you convinced now, after reading me the riot act?" He gave her a side smile, displaying his deep dimple again.

"OK, OK. I'll ride with you." She smiled. "But you have to bring me right back. My mom is picking me up within a half hour."

He pointed to the seat on the motorcycle and provided a helmet for her. She could see he'd come prepared. As Ricardo accelerated, Radiance felt the breeze against her face and the secret enjoyment of wrapping her arms around Ricardo. After that day, he picked her up after school for the next two weeks.

They always rode to a nearby park; then they sat on a bench and talked. She loved that he was a gentleman. She had mixed emotions, sensing she was growing fond of him. She could not stop smiling after he drove away.

Ricardo convinced Radiance to get a small tattoo. The date was set for Friday after school—she told her mom that she was going home with Makayla. As arranged, Ricardo picked her up after school, and they rode on his motorcycle to his studio.

"Would you like something to drink?" Ricardo asked her.

"A bottle of water, if you have one," she said timidly. It was clear she was nervous about getting the tattoo.

"What about a little weed?" He lit a joint and held it out for her.

"I don't smoke," she said shyly.

"I bet you never tried it before."

"Never!"

"A puff or two will relax you and ease the pain slightly."

"I'm not so sure I want to. I don't know what it will do to me."

"I won't let anything happen to you," he promised.

"OK, but just a couple of puffs. Remember I have to go home after this."

"I got you. There's enough time for it to wear off. Just relax."

After a few puffs, Radiance began to feel lightheaded. As Ricardo started drawing the tattoo, it burned a little, but, just like he said, the weed dulled the pain. When he finished the tattoo, his body brushed up against hers, and she started to perspire in unwanted places.

He bent forward toward her lips and began kissing her. Surprisingly, she responded with open lips. The next thing she knew, his hands were touching uninvited areas. She fell limp in his arms, but in her racing mind, she was fighting the urge to continue. She mentally heard her mom's voice and pulled away.

He looked into her eyes and sensed her uneasiness. "You OK?"

"No," she said, breathing heavily and pulling herself together. "I think I better leave now."

He stepped back and took her by the hand. "I'm sorry. I didn't mean to come on so strong, but I really like you, and I'm very attracted to you. I can see you're different from the other girls I've met. I won't force you into anything you don't want to do."

"I thought it was clear that we were just friends," Radiance said.

She grabbed her things, and the two of them quietly headed back to the school.

As she got off the motorcycle, he said, "I hope I can see you again."

Radiance barely nodded and then handed him her helmet. She watched as he sped away.

She looked at her tattoo and wanted to smile. She felt excited, but at the same time, she knew she'd taken a big risk by smoking and lying to her mother. With blurred vision, she knew she could not call her mom. The only person who would understand was her Auntie Ellona, whom she affectionately called "Auntie E." She dialed Ellona's number.

After several rings, Ellona answered.

"Hi, Auntie E."

"Radiance. I am surprised to hear from you on a Friday evening. Where are you?"

"I'm at school. I need a ride home. Can you come get me?"

"You sound a little different. Is everything OK?"

"I need a ride home."

"OK. I'll be there in ten minutes."

Ellona jumped into her blue Mini Cooper S convertible and headed to the school. She spotted Radiance sitting on the curb. When Radiance climbed into the car, the familiar scent hit Ellona's nose.

When she noticed Radiance's red eyes, she began to ask questions. "Are you OK?"

"I am now. I had an—unexpected experience." Radiance speech was slurred.

"You want to talk about it?"

"I got my first tattoo," Radiance said, showing Ellona the small angel on her ankle.

"That's beautiful. I take it your parents don't know about it."

"No, Auntie E." Radiance then explained the weed and the tattoo. "I should have known better than to smoke a joint. I don't smoke cigarettes, and I didn't like it. I was curious and wanted to seem cool and fit in, like all the other teens. I didn't know it would have this kind of effect on me. I never get to go anywhere, let alone be with someone who likes me. Please don't look at me like that, Auntie E." Radiance began to cry.

"Sounds like there's a lot going on inside that you're not talking to anyone about," Ellona said. "I understand it's not easy being a teenager these days, but it could help to talk to someone about your feelings."

"That's why I called you. I knew you would understand."

"I see. He didn't hurt you, did he?"

"No."

"Where did you meet him?" Ellona asked.

"He's a friend of my friend Makayla. He comes around on his motorcycle after school each day with her boyfriend, Tommy. He's also a dancer and got accepted to Juilliard."

"But he paints tattoos for all the teenagers? Was this your first encounter with him?"

"No, I rode with him on his motorcycle a few times after school.

We go to a nearby park, where we sit and talk, but this was the first time he kissed me."

"Is that all that happened?"

"It happened just like I told you. He held me in his arms, and we were getting really heated, and then I pulled away. He was a gentleman. He respected me when I said let's stop and didn't force himself on me."

"Then there's nothing to worry about."

"But I took a chance that could have turned out badly. I started feeling things moving in a strange direction when my body started heating up and—"

"OK, I understand. Nothing happened, right?"

"Right!"

"Good. Boys are attractive to pretty girls like you and especially to pretty, *nice* girls. When you hang out, one thing can lead to another unless you set some boundaries. Does Grace know about him?"

"Absolutely not!"

"You and Grace need to talk. But maybe not today. You don't want her to see you like this, I'm sure."

"No, I don't. We have small talks, but for the most part, they're not about me. They're about the most immediate thing—the school and Mom and Dad's work. She is always busy."

"I see."

"He's also older than me."

"How much older?" Ellona inquired.

"Two years; he's sixteen. His name is Ricardo, and he's Latino."

"It sounds like you have some feelings for him."

"He's the first boy I have been attracted to. I *cannot* tell Mom what happened today—with the smoking or about the tattoo. She thinks I'm a perfect little angel. Besides, I lied to her and said I was going to Makayla's after school. I just didn't know it would turn out this way."

"I understand completely. Like I said, you and Grace need to talk. Believe me, I had my share of experiences at your age, none of which was as simple as your story. Let me talk to your mom first. The last thing she needs is to worry about you. She's been stressed lately and would blow a fuse at the thought of this. You know how precious you are to her. I can't even begin to think about your father knowing any of this."

"Yeah, I know."

"I'll let you off on this corner," Ellona said, bringing her car to a stop. When you get home, go straight to your room. Take a nice hot shower and listen to some music. The feeling will eventually wear off, and you'll be able to sleep."

"Thanks, Auntie E. I knew you would understand. I love you." Radiance gave her a big hug.

~

Radiance quickly passed through the entrance hall and up the stairs. Grace was sitting in the living room and got only a flash of her presence. She called out to Radiance from the bottom of the stairway. Radiance replied with a "Hey, Mom" before closing her door. She didn't want to face her mother's acute sense of smell. She dialed Makayla's number, hoping she would pick up.

"What's up, girl? You still at Ricardo's?"

"No. We cut the evening short."

"Why?"

Radiance gave a recap of the incident.

"Girl! Sounds like you almost got some." Makayla giggled.

"It was not like that at all. It got heated, but I came to my senses and told him I had to go. He was a perfect gentleman."

"Has your mom seen your tattoo?"

"Heck, no! I went straight to my room. She would have a fit and then tell my dad, and he would go looking for the poor boy. God forbid." She laughed. "I'm getting ready to take a hot bath and then listen to some music."

"So you'll be ready for your second tattoo soon?"

"Ha! I don't think so. This one still hurts." She laughed.

"It will wear off, and you'll want another one soon; I guarantee you. Would you like to go to the mall tomorrow?"

"I can't. Remember I told you that Javier and I are participating in an art competition tomorrow."

"Oh yes. Right. Well, be the winner. I'll see you at school on Monday.

"Thanks. See you then."

CHAPTER

13

Art Competition

The Wellington Holmes Art Academy was the sponsor and producer of The Future Is Bright art competition, held at the College of Fine Arts in Harlem. The lobby was filled with bubbling students, checking out the registration area for their entry board. Radiance and Javier entered on a dual project and felt destined to win. Javier had created a unique ceramic piece that Radiance had painted. There were multiple new categories this year, and one was a complete surprise to Radiance.

While looking at the entry board, Radiance felt a soft tap on her shoulder. Her eyes widened and mouth dropped open when she saw Ricardo standing behind her. Javier noticed the mutual attraction between the two and became very suspicious. Radiance spoke softly to him as she walked toward her father, Wellington, and brother, Javier.

"Radiance, I want to apologize to you."

"You did already. Why are you here?" Radiance whispered.

"Why are you being so secretive?"

"Sorry. I'm just staying focused."

"I didn't know you were entered into this competition," Ricardo said.

"Yes. You know which school I attend—or maybe you don't know my father, Wellington Holmes."

"Wellington Holmes? I didn't know he was your father. I'm familiar with his work."

They had reached Wellington, who asked, "Who is your friend?"

"This is Ricardo," Radiance said.

"Nice to meet you." Wellington shook his hand firmly and looked him up and down before stepping away.

"Why are you here, Ricardo?" Radiance asked again.

"I'm here for the competition. They added a new category for tattoo artists. The prizes are too good to ignore."

"You're painting live tattoos?" she asked, just as Javier approached them.

"Who is painting tattoos?" Javier asked. "I want one!"

"This is my brother, Javier. We entered the competition on a dual project in the visual arts category."

"Hey," Javier said, giving Ricardo a fist bump.

"Nice meeting you," Javier said. "I'll check you out later to get that tattoo."

"All right, man." After Javier walked away, Ricardo said, "Radiance, I am sorry for the way things turned out. I didn't mean to upset you. I should have approached you differently. Can you forgive me?"

"Yes, I forgive you, and I also take responsibility."

"Why don't we talk about it after school on Monday?"

"We'll see about that after the competition."

"Why is that?" he asked.

"After we smoke you in this competition, you may not want to see me for a few days. But good luck to you." She grinned.

"Oh! That's what's up!" Ricardo laughed as he walked away.

And the winner is—?

CHAPTER

14

Ellona's Advice

Ellona, a crème honey-colored, five-foot-seven beauty with straight, long brown hair and a big personality, had met Grace over ten years ago when Grace had visited Ellona's spa for a professional massage. She was of African-Native American descent and socially from a different side of the tracks than Grace—as an only child, Grace had been raised in a loving two-parent home, with all her needs met.

As a young teen, Ellona ran away from a broken home and lived a precarious street life. At age twenty-one, she was rescued by a Christian woman who changed her life. After several years, Ellona received training as a certified masseuse and opened her own business, Spa 52, located on the Upper East Side of Manhattan. Through Grace's visits to Spa 52, a trusted relationship developed, and they became as close as sisters. Ellona knew she could talk to Grace about anything, but this time was different. It is sensitive to talk to anyone about her own child.

Ellona sat in her car outside Grace's house, trying to force her fingers to call the number. She prayed that Grace's heart would be tender enough to receive her strong words and that it would bridge the gap between mother and daughter.

"Can we talk?" Ellona asked Grace.

"Yes. Do you want me to come to the spa?"

"You don't have to go that far. Open your front door. I'm right outside."

"Oh, this must be good. I'm the one who usually comes to you to talk." Grace went to the door and waved Ellona into the house.

Ellona walked into the living room and paced the floor. "Is anybody here?"

"It is just you and me. What's up, girl? You're usually at the spa with customers."

"Yes, I know, but my heart is heavy."

"Sounds serious," Grace said, noting the lines in Ellona's face.

"It's Radiance I want to talk about."

"Girl, don't talk in code. Just tell me straight out. Have a seat."

"Seasons of your success will be futile unless you take a break for your family. You have a chance to act before it comes crashing down on you."

"Are you trying to prophesy to me?"

"No. I'm just saying that some things are going on, and you're too busy to notice."

Grace became alarmed by Ellona's indirect approach. "What about Radiance?"

"No need to panic. As a teenager, she doesn't know how to talk to you."

"She can talk to me anytime," Grace said.

"No, she cannot! You're way too busy. Teens need their mothers, and if their mothers aren't available, then they go to someone else—in this case, me, Auntie E. She called and I listened. You better be glad she did. At her age, she needs you, Grace. You need to hear what is going on with her. Fourteen years old ain't no joke. Seize and embrace this opportunity while you can. I would be counting my blessings if I had a daughter like Radiance."

Grace was stunned. She tried to recall the last time she and Radiance had had a heart-to-heart talk. It was some time ago. She frowned. "I'd be wrong if I didn't admit to a twinge of jealousy that she talked to you rather than me."

Grace reflected on her incident with her painting *Angel in Disguise*, remembering when she tried to talk to Wellington and tell him the truth about the painting, but he was too busy for her. That resulted in a decision Grace later regretted. Now, she looked up at Ellona. "I hope Radiance hasn't made a bad decision."

"Let's just say she made a decision, but it's something you can deal with."

"Tell me what is going *on*," Grace said, raising her voice a little.

"Teenage stuff."

Grace raised her eyebrows. "Be more specific, girlfriend. There's a lot of 'teenage stuff' going on."

"Breathe, Grace. She hasn't done anything she'll regret. She's developing feelings for a boy, and he's a tattoo artist."

"Oh boy, not an artist!"

"Yes, he is. He is even going to Juilliard next year. Her friend Makayla has a tattoo, and Radiance wanted one too, so she got one." Ellona proceeded to tell Grace what had happened and then waited for Grace's response.

"What!?" Grace looked at Ellona in disbelief.

"It isn't the end of the world. All the kids have them."

"Why is she talking to you and not me?"

"Like I said, it's because I will listen and not judge her. She's a good girl. In fact, she is a gem! I would give anything to have a child like Radiance. Believe me, there are some wild ones out there, and you are blessed that she's not one of them. She's feeling some kind of way, and it is not a bad time for you to step up your motherly duties," Ellona declared with a straight face.

"Wow, it's like that, huh?" Grace said, clearly offended. "I guess I shouldn't be too surprised. As a child, her curiosity had no limits."

"Yes, like that!" Ellona snapped her fingers. "I didn't want to point it out like that, but I feel, as friends, we should be able to give each other an honest assessment."

"I'm listening so stop lecturing me," Grace snapped back.

"You need to have a one-on-one with her more often. Otherwise, you are going to lose her along the way, and she will get advice from her friends. At least she's venting and trusting me to listen. These kids are faced with a lot of peer pressure. Social media and the internet dictate the examples for them to live by. That's why they make suspect choices. Teenagers need parental guidance, whether they want it or not. You need to hear how she is thinking. Obviously, this is a season to change what you do with her and not be afraid of the change. I told her I would have a talk with you," Ellona said, trying to soften the hard blow.

"Wow. I guess I have been in my own world. I didn't realize I haven't been on my job with my child. How do you think I should approach her?"

"Remember the talks with your mother. Reflect on that and do *you*, but listen to her. Teens today need secure relationships and the right mental attitude for developing their moral checks. What helps is having parental support, and many teens don't have it. I didn't! If need be, I'll be here as your accountable partner."

"Thanks, girl. Once again, you are an angel in disguise, and I appreciate you. After this talk, I need a total body massage." Grace grimaced.

"Come to the spa tomorrow, and I'll take care of you."

"Yeah. You do still owe me."

"For what?" They laughed and embraced.

Ellona

CHAPTER

15

Quality Time

Grace looked up at the cloudless blue sky and felt the warmth of the Florida sun and the ocean breeze on her face. She inhaled deeply. This weekend, she had put her world aside to concentrate on her most precious asset—her daughter, Radiance. She looked at Radiance—her brown skin and black silky hair pulled up in a ponytail; her slender body in a size 4 yellow bikini. Radiance was a natural beauty, without an ounce of pretense or vanity. Grace gave her a warm smile as she pushed the sand with her toes in Radiance's direction. Grace reminded herself that she and Wellington had done something right in raising their daughter. Their mother-daughter talk time together was to be used to develop a new way to talk and to help Grace to develop important listening skills.

Radiance sat up in her beach chair and faced Grace. "Mom, thank you for making me come this weekend."

"I knew we needed time together, and since we both love the ocean, I figured what better place than a Florida beach?"

A moment of silence passed before Radiance spoke again.

"Mom, I want to tell you something, but you have to promise not to overreact."

"OK." Grace sat up and braced herself, hoping it was not something outside of the news that Ellona had stunned her with.

"I got a tattoo."

"Yes, I noticed it. Ellona told me about it. I know most of the kids probably have them, right?"

"Yes, Mom. What do you think?" Radiance gleefully displayed her left ankle.

"I like the angel. Did it hurt?"

"Yes, a little."

"When did you get it?"

"A few weeks ago," she said sheepishly.

"Can I ask why you didn't show me right away?"

Radiance had a hard time articulating her feelings. "I was scared, I guess. I know I probably should have asked you first, but you and Dad are so strict. I wasn't sure how to approach you."

"Oh, I see. I can see that we really need this time to talk."

"I want to be more like the other kids and fit in."

"You don't have to try and fit in, baby. Just be you."

"But I feel different. I don't seem like a natural fit."

"That's because you *are* different. You are unique, all by yourself. You remind me lot of myself when I was in high school. I chose to be alone and stayed to myself. I wish now that I had mingled more."

"I'm finally meeting more friends now and starting to enjoy myself more," Radiance said, producing a wide smile.

"I heard!"

"I guess Auntie E told you everything?"

"Yes, she did. I'm not surprised about the tattoo. I was a little hurt by the way she called me out on not doing my job, and a little hurt that you didn't come to me first. A mother wants to be the first to know about her own child." Grace pouted.

"Oh, Mom, I'm sorry about that. I didn't mean to hurt you."

"It's not your fault. I'm good. That's why I thought it would be nice for us to spend time alone."

"I think I learned my lesson about keeping things from you. I'm also sorry for that. I'm learning quickly about making bad decisions."

"I am proud of you for making the ones you have made up to this point. Be careful about the friends you choose and the situations you get into. Communication is important. Your dad and I have busy careers, but you and Javier should always come first. I know we can do better, and we plan on changing that."

"I would like that." Radiance flashed a warm smile.

"Mom, you know I love you. I always want to respect you and Dad, but I'm growing up, and I'm hoping y'all will unloose that noose a little bit. I'm sure Auntie E told you about Ricardo. He's a nice guy." Radiance took a deep breath and then said, "He's a tattoo artist, and next year, he will be a Juilliard student."

"Oh yes, I heard. Haven't you listened to my stories about artists?" Grace joked. "I take it he's the one who painted your tattoo?"

"Now, Mom, calm down. Don't bash artists. Ricardo is an interesting person. You married one too, remember?" She smiled. "Don't judge him before you meet him."

"You're right. But, little girl, you cannot compare your experience with mine. I was in college when I met your father. Wait—you haven't even started dating anybody. I cannot protect you from everything and everyone, but it's our responsibility to give you some guidelines. I love you, baby girl, and that's what I want to do. Let's just talk and take things one step at a time." Grace leaned over and kissed Radiance on her forehead.

"I understand, Mom. Now, can you tell me the infamous story again?"

"Which story, dear?"

"You know. The love story between you and Dad. The artist you met and married. Can Daddy dance?" She chuckled.

"Yes, he can cut a step. Your dad has told you that story a million times. I don't know why you want to hear it again."

"I like hearing the girl's version, plus your story of 'sheroism,'" Radiance said with a laugh.

"Well, I don't know about all that sheroism stuff. I will tell you that your dad exaggerates the story a great deal. But it is true that he swept me off my feet."

"How old were you?"

"Nineteen. Up to that point, I'd never had a serious boyfriend."

"Never? That sounds like me."

"It sounds like you have already had encounters that I never had. Anyway, in my freshman year of college, your father was my art professor. He was a well-known artist whose work I had followed. On my first day of class, when I entered the classroom and saw him standing at the desk—girl, I was a hot mess! As the story goes, I fainted!"

"Mom, that's hard to believe. You are always so cool. I cannot imagine you hitting the floor."

"I did, darling. Eventually, I got my act together. But I think the love bug bit me when I hit the floor, and I did not know it. At first, he paid attention to me; then, out of the blue, he went cold and ignored me for months. But one beautiful day, he could not hold out any longer and came looking for me. We started dating, and he eventually proposed, and we got married. When I entered the world as an artist's wife, I was immature. I was a quiet soul and didn't enjoy the limelight of a notable artist or of an artist's companion. Your father, on the other hand, loved the public attention and was very charismatic. He had a rising career. I was developing my own motif as an artist, but not nearly on the level of your father. There were art exhibitions, agents, decisions, losses, and mistakes. Speaking of which, I made a big mistake that turned our relationship upside down. There was an evil guy named Azul who tried to blackmail me, but he didn't get away with it. He eventually died in a car crash. I was under a lot of stress at that time and lost your older sister. But God blessed us again with another child. You! The rest is history."

"Mom, you're leaving out some good stuff, like that time you pointed a gun at someone, and you escaped death."

"I'm skipping over that drama. Like I said, the rest is history. I defended your dad's legacy, and to this day, I would not change a thing. All I went through was for us, but I did not do it alone. God and my angels in disguise were with me. That was then; this is now!"

"Mom, you always say that. You are amazing! I hope I remain as humble as you when I grow up and blow up."

"Baby girl, you are all that right now and much more. I want you to have fun in your teenage years. When I was your age, my mom and dad gave me permission to be me. I hope I'm doing the same for you. I want to meet Ricardo when we get back home, but I want you to remember how old you are. More importantly, I want us to be close. Your dad feels the same way. I am sorry for being selfish with my time. We are going to make some changes, and I want open lines of communication between us. One thing that helped me in my teens—and helps me still to this day—is the sound wisdom I received from my mom."

"I admire how close you and Granny are."

"She loves me, and I trust her advice. That's the relationship I want for us."

"I want that too, Mom."

"I promise to do better."

SEASON 3
Changed Attitudes

CHAPTER

16

Rediscovered Purpose

"**H**ey, girl! Wait up." Makayla stopped Radiance as she walked by. "You been avoiding me or something?"

"I have several tests, and I'm also taking a few more classes. It's really tough, and it's taking up my time."

"Really? It seems more like you sort of fell out with me. I see you in class; then you hurry away. You don't call me on the phone anymore."

"I was trying to find a way to tell you—nothing personal, but I cannot hang with y'all anymore."

"What do you mean? You could have just told us. You just left us hanging, girl."

"After that day at Ricardo's, I realized I'm sort of out of my lane. So much happened so fast, and I was freaked out and broke my moral compass. I was doing some things that felt uncomfortable. I forgot that I am only fourteen."

"Yeah, I kind of figured that by the way you told me you stormed out of Ricardo's house that day. But nobody made you do anything."

"Right, he was a perfect gentleman, but it still scares me because I really don't know Ricardo. Almost anything could have happened to me as a young female. I didn't even know you well enough to know if you would have had my back if he wasn't cool. You know, what I mean?"

"I get it. But you could have talked to me about it."

"I am not into all that. I don't judge you, but I got a purpose for my life and I want to stay on track. I am trying to go to college in a few years. Heaven forbid I should end up pregnant."

"Yeah, well, that's some years away."

"I know, but I don't need distractions."

"I probably could learn some things from you. I knew you were different, and that's why I was drawn to you. I still want to be friends with you. Ricardo was starting to like you. I think you broke his heart."

"Broke his heart? He is tripping. I'm too young to date or even know what love is. If he likes me and wants to date me, he will have to wait."

"Ah, you are talking like a mature young lady right now." Makayla smiled. "My boyfriend says he loves me too, but I ain't ready for that either."

"Really? You, with reservations? I could not tell by the way y'all be kissing."

"Nothing harmful in that."

"Yeah, right. But that leads to more, especially if you can't handle smoking. You know what I mean?"

"Girl, I am fifteen. I know that," Makayla snapped.

"Ricardo is cute and everything. I also felt a little something, but I had to check myself. He's much older than me. What happened at his place left me questioning what I was doing there. It is not the environment I want to be in."

"Whatever, girl." Makayla turned to leave.

"It ain't *whatever*," Radiance said, grabbing Makayla by the hand to face her. "I needed you as a friend, but friends keep each other safe. That was not safe. What if I would have gotten caught smoking that joint? Huh? I need a sidekick who has my back. We are blessed to be in a top-notch school with a good future ahead of us. No hard feelings or anything. It may be that we no longer have anything in common. I hope you don't throw your chances away by trying to be the most popular girl, or into drugs and boys. I have plenty of time to date, but right now, I want to focus on school and my art."

"My mom says I can do anything if I put my mind to it. I will succeed—just watch me. Let me know if you change your mind; then we can talk. We are doing some real talk now!" Makayla sashayed away.

"Did your mom also tell you there are consequences for the choices you make?" Radiance shouted after her.

CHAPTER

17

Village Talk

"**I** feel like she blindsided me," Radiance cried to Ellona and Grace. Ruth, Radiance's grandmother, was also on the zoom call.

"She's the classmate you've been hanging around with for a few months, and you didn't have any idea she was a little different—maybe on the wild side?" Grace asked.

"Mom, you don't understand. She's one of my friends at school."

"Or do you mean that she's the cutest and most popular one in the class?"

"Yes, that too. But nobody else reached out or befriended me."

"What about you? Did you reach out to anyone?"

Radiance slumped in her chair.

"I understand, child. I was the same way; I stayed to myself. I called us together to talk about this situation, which seems to have left you a little down. Granny and Auntie E were concerned too, and we just wanted to listen to you and support you with some love and counsel. We want to learn from you too, precious."

"I know, Mom. I feel good about that. I was happy to finally have a friend. Makayla and I were building a strong relationship and having fun. She never smoked or took a drink or any of that in front of me. How was I to know she would bring me into a situation like that?" Radiance asked.

"That's what teenagers do," Ellona said. "They get to know you but don't tell you everything about themselves at first. The leader can easily sway others in a slick kind of way. Based on what you told me, she sounds a little fast for you anyway. Am I right?"

"Didn't you say her mom works all the time, and at fifteen she's left to make some decisions on her own?" Ruth inquired.

Radiance grimaced before replying. "Yes, Auntie and Granny."

"See? There you go," Ruth said. "You really don't know her at all, but you know she is allowed to go some places you aren't. That should have told you something right there. Young lady, you are blessed with a family to back you up with sound advice and guidance."

"Yes, and I wish I'd had a mom who did that for me," Ellona added. "Unfortunately, I had a rough upbringing, and I left home in my early teens and made some bad decisions. I paid for them, and I learned many valuable lessons that changed my life."

"I am thankful to have all of you, even if right now, it seems a little over the top." Radiance smiled. "I know you care, and I appreciate you. I am sorry I let all of you down."

"You are going to have some growing pains," Grace consoled her. "This time, you escaped, and you made a wise decision to put on some brakes at that moment and to ask Ricardo to take you home."

"Now, tell us what you learned from this." Ruth said.

"Granny, I learned to rely on my values and the God inside of me when I get a warning that something is not quite right."

"What about your choice of friends?" Ellona asked.

"That too. I need to choose my friends more carefully and have real talks every step of the way."

"Yes, but the most important part is that not only did you listen to your inner feelings, but you acted on them," Grace reminded her. "You have several girls in your classes. Why not get to know them? Art can be the basis of your relationships to start conversations with them. I was the same way. I know I'm preaching to the choir." She smiled.

"Mom—"

"You know I'm right about it. But let me say this: We are proud of the decision you made. It shows you are maturing into a fine young lady."

"I am extremely proud of my granddaughter. Radiance, I want you to do something for me," Ruth said.

"What, Granny?"

"I want you to start calling me more often so we can develop a closer relationship. I will keep your conversations confidential, as I do with your mom. I know I'm way out in California, but I'm a phone call away. I don't know much about teenagers today, but I am willing to learn and to impart some wisdom into your life. By the way, I heard you and Javier aren't hanging out much. How come?"

"I know, Granny. I can do better. We have different paths, but he's always trying to be friends with me. I don't know what's wrong with me."

"You just need to come out of your shell of wanting to be alone," Grace said. "I get it."

"I think after that incident with Ricardo, I don't want to even look at a boy, not even my brother."

"That's not the right attitude, young lady," Ruth said. "You can take the lessons learned and move on. Besides, what happened with Ricardo was not Javier's fault."

"You two are growing up and have to learn how to talk to one another. He is your brother. He loves you, and I know that you love him too," Grace reminded her.

"I guess you're right."

"You need to do better than try," Ruth agreed.

"And don't let Auntie E be the only one you talk to." Grace chuckled.

"Don't hate!" Ellona said.

They all laughed.

"Thank you all for loving me and supporting me. I really mean that from my heart."

"You know you are my favorite niece, so you can call me anytime." Ellona looked at Grace and put up her hand.

"I know, Auntie E," Radiance said. "I'm your favorite niece and your *only* niece."

They laughed.

"Ladies, thanks for being available. Talk with y'all later," Grace said.

They ended the Zoom call by blowing kisses. The ladies exhaled, realizing they had accomplished a renewed relationship with Radiance.

Ruth Green

CHAPTER

18

Art Matters Too

"I am amazed that so many great artists were selected for the Works Progress Administration, also known as the WPA, like Jacob Lawrence, Elizabeth Catlett, and Charles White, who benefited from the historic US government program that was created in 1939," Javier explained during the class discussion.

"Who can tell me during which presidency this program was created?" Wellington asked.

Ava raised her hand. "Franklin D. Roosevelt. His wife, Eleanor, created it around 1939 to 1943."

"Who was it created for?" Wellington asked the class.

"It was for the unemployed," Quinn replied.

"I am looking for more information. For what purpose?" Wellington said.

"It was a program funded by the federal government to help unemployed artists of color create public and private art. It was also supposed to unite a nation in turmoil," Radiance replied.

"Right. Who was the director who got Congress' attention to initiate this program?"

"Harry L. Hopkins," Quinn replied. "Harry and his staff argued on behalf of these talented people who were unemployed, like writers, artists, musicians, those in the theater, even laborers and farmers."

"Great, Quinn. Let me give you an example. Artists were employed to decorate buildings with murals, and they built sculptures," Wellington said.

"Didn't his team get Congress to allocate 7 percent of WPA funding to employ those groups?" Areema asked.

"You are correct," Wellington replied.

"Also, the idea behind the project was to bring art to the masses, so America would have a common cultural vocabulary. These programs were considered progressive for that era," Radiance added. She smiled because she had studied and could engage in the conversation.

"Good discussion, class. This is just an introduction on this era. For homework, I want each of you to consider your discipline and area of expertise. If you were alive during that time frame, what would you contribute artistically? How would you determine your art's cultural and public benefit?"

"Do you mean we need to paint, or create a song, or act out a part in a play?" Javier asked.

"Exactly! Also, be prepared to present your work clearly for public benefit," Wellington added. "The only way artists get recognition is when they produce work. If you want to be considered great, consider your work important enough to display publicly. Before we dismiss, I have words of encouragement for you. God has given all of you gifts and made you unique. He is the greatest creator. View your talent and gifts as something special. You are the only one who can do what you do, and we need everybody. Just like a band. There are the drums, the horns, and the strings. They all make up the melody. Your input is needed. Art soothes, and people need healing and encouragement. It also makes them want to create."

"My mom says she knows I'm talented, but I should also think about going to college and getting a real job," Janise said.

"Believe me, I heard that a million times." Wellington laughed. "There is nothing wrong with getting an education. I became a college art professor. I now run a multimillion-dollar academy, and as an independent international artist, my income is satisfying. My recommendation is to follow what you love and keep your passion. Talking it over with your parents is important too, so don't skip that step."

"Professor, sometimes I get discouraged because I don't know if I will be able to make a good living as an artist." Areema frowned.

"Most people who do well love what they do. What other people will pay for is always the big question. Trust your gift and persevere, and do not give up. It's important for you to practice your craftmanship. Many artists do not practice or study the history of art and artifacts. Your imagination is key to your uniqueness and originality. OK, class, that wraps it up for the day. See you on Monday." Wellington then dismissed them but asked Javier and Radiance to stay behind.

They looked at each other with questions on their faces.

"Hey, guys. How are you both doing? Y'all are too separate to be living in the same house."

"Well, she has her schedule, and I have mine," Javier said. "And besides, she stays in her room and acts like she doesn't want to be bothered with me."

Radiance rolled her eyes. "I never said that."

"You didn't have to. Your attitude speaks for itself."

"That is why we are having this conversation," Wellington said, holding up his hand to quiet both. "Your mom and I can see what is happening. This is the perfect time, while you are young, to start communicating and developing a relationship. It is important to us.

You are talented, but on a personal level, you are both selfish. We are counting on you to work out your differences and decide to like, even love, each other."

"I don't hate him. Do you know how irritating boys are?"

"Doesn't sound like love to me," Wellington said.

"OK, Dad. Guys never understand how a girl feels."

"I am feeling you. I just know you can do better."

"Yeah, but you and Mom have your own separate studios, and you travel one week and her the next," Radiance said before she knew it.

"Yes, but we are grown, and that is a different situation. We are artists and we do need our separate space, but nothing separates our love as a couple. Likewise, there should be no space that separates the love for a sibling."

Radiance gave a half smile to show her agreement. She picked up her books and walked outside the large classroom. Out of the corner of her eye, she saw movement and recognized Ricardo.

He approached her slowly. "Hey."

"Hey, yourself," she said with trepidation. "How've you been?"

"I'm OK. How about you?"

"I'm good," Radiance said, grappling for the right words to say. "I'm surprised to see you."

"Is that good or bad?"

"It's OK."

"I just want to know if you're still mad at me," Ricardo said.

"No, I never was mad at you."

"Can we go somewhere to talk?"

"I can't right now. I have to go home."

"Well, can I call you?"

Radiance smiled but didn't respond.

"I know you've avoided me. I want to talk with you and get a few things straight. And I still want to be friends. I'm sorry for the way things went down. I know I got ahead of myself. I respect your age and won't be coming on to you like that anymore."

"Thank you for saying that. I forgot myself too. I really didn't know you very well. I don't want to be just an artist and tattoo designer's plaything. I didn't know how to approach you after that day."

"I know. Me neither."

They both turned to see Javier walking their way.

"Hey, man. What's up?" Ricardo said.

"I'm good. Radiance, are you ready to go?" Javier asked.

"Yes, give me a moment. I'll catch up with you."

"You didn't answer my question. Can I call you later?" Ricardo asked again.

"Yes, that would be OK." She walked away with a half-smile and turned to see the big grin on his face as well.

∼

Later that evening, Javier peeked into Radiance's room to talk with her.

"Hey. What are you doing?"

"You see I am busy," she said, perturbed by his presence.

"You want to go to the Metropolitan Museum tomorrow? We have that assignment to turn in next week. Maybe we can look at some of the artists' work Dad talked about."

"Nah, I'm busy."

"You're not doing anything but painting, girl. You stay in your room for hours. Don't you get bored? Come on and go with me." He pulled her sleeve to move her. "We never spend time together. We have to start sometime, like Dad said. Besides, I want to spend time with you."

"All right. Don't be so pushy."

"It's going to benefit both of us. We need to know our art history so we can also talk about that in class. Dad isn't playing; he's stepping it up."

"I know you're right," Radiance said. "

"Unless you have other plans with that Ricardo guy? Who is he anyway? When and where did you meet him?"

"Stay out of my business, boy! What time are we going?"

"Oh, you gonna do me like that and avoid my question?"

"You are just so nosy!" She pushed him. "I'll tell you tomorrow when we go to the museum."

"Yeah, I can't wait to hear."

"Don't get smart. I said I would go with you, so get out of my room." She shoved him again.

"Sis, I am the greatest big-brother protector you'll ever know. You just aren't taking advantage of it".

"Boy, you are crazy." She grinned. "OK. Now go." She waved him away.

SEASON 4
Ambitious Encounters

CHAPTER

19

Liquid Art Intelligence (LAI)

The phone jingled its familiar tone. "Grace, it's Monica. How's Wellington?"

"He's good. The past few weeks he has been sleeping like a baby."

"That's what I want to hear. Now, I have something *you'll* want to hear."

"Good news, I hope."

"It's excellent news. The battery of tests and trials for Liquid Art Intelligence is finished. Our team devised a product that will be hard for anyone to duplicate. The 'secret sauce' lies within a rare mineral found in Bolivia. It will cut down on the international stolen art crisis and make criminals think twice about replicating intellectual property. I think I've mentioned that the attorneys believe Switzerland is the best place to register this product because there is more protection here."

"This is surreal."

"Yes, it is finally ready. We found a company who can manufacture the product at a reasonable cost. I also love the logo design that Wellington created for the product."

"I am so excited! You know there is no way I could have accomplished this without my new angel team—you, Tracey, and Georgie."

"Girl, please. We love the process."

"What are our next steps?" Grace asked.

"We have applied for the patent and will do some sampling. That will take time. Once that is finished and the application is approved, we are on to production and marketing. That's it!"

Grace felt faint and dropped the phone.

"Grace? Grace? Are you there?" Monica asked when she heard the telephone drop.

"Sorry. I heard you. I think I temporarily blanked out. This is overwhelming, and I don't know what to say."

"Stay with me on this, girl. This is no time to faint. There is still a lot of work to do."

They laughed.

Grace gathered herself. "OK, I'm back. Just a little while longer for the approval, but it is exciting seeing a dream come true. I cannot wait to tell Wellington."

"You and Wellington are trailblazers in the art industry. This will be a big part of your legacy. Realistically, you know we can only control so much of the criminal activity out there. But this is a good start. The art community will be singing your name, girl!"

"Accolades and awards are nice, but I don't need all that. It doesn't mean as much as making a difference in the community. I just want to be useful. Monica, thank you for your dedication to this project. It means a lot."

"We are in this together. The best part is, God gets the glory!"

With the release of the Liquid Art Intelligence Product a year and half later, Grace, Wellington, and all involved entered a new level of financial security, but it also brought enemies.

LAI, an aerosol spray, was to be applied to the back of paintings. It gave off a luminous light to determine artwork authenticity. The feminine design of the plastic bottle was similar to a perfume spray bottle. The sizes ranged from small to large, representing an important development in the history of the product.

LAI was warmly welcomed by many museums. Some of the first to implement the tool were the Museum of Modern Art, New York; Musée D'Orsay, Paris; the Art Institute of Chicago; the Museum of Qin Terracotta Warriors and Horses, Xi'an, China; Zeitz Museum of Contemporary Art Africa, Cape Town, South Africa; the British Museum, London, England; State Hermitage Museum, St. Petersburg, Florida; the National Gallery, London; The Musée du Louvre, Paris; High Museum, Atlanta, Georgia; Norton Simon Museum, Pasadena, California; San Francisco Museum of Modern Art; the Van Gogh Museum, Amsterdam; the Getty Center, Los Angeles; and the National Gallery of Arts, Washington, DC.

CHAPTER

20

Exposed Art Fraud

New York's twenty-year veteran detective, Carlos Ramos, was a nonchalant mild-mannered man who stood five feet nine, but he was lauded as a giant in law enforcement. His life career was dedicated to uncovering art theft, catching the criminals, and bringing them to justice. He was highly respected and recently had been promoted to Special Agent, an international position with the FBI Art Crime team.

He removed his famously worn black hat, scratched his thinning curly black hair, and wrote on his notepad. He could not believe the latest bizarre rise in stolen art and art insurance fraud claims. Within the last year, more art insurance claims began surfacing, leading him to open a sophisticated investigation. Qualified art specialists were called in to help. Switzerland's cantonal police probe began by looking at multiple galleries that were missing paintings. The Johansson Gallery in Switzerland was one of those being investigated. Their client list included Ty Hamilton as the top patron. Special Agent Ramos worked closely with the Johanssons to see if there was a connection between Ty and art insurance fraud, but they could find none. The FBI Art Crime team and the Swiss police worked closely together to recover some of the stolen paintings from galleries but didn't recover all. Special Agent Ramos dialed Grace's number to deliver the mystifying news.

"Hi, Grace. How have you been?"

"Fine. What about you?"

"I'm good. How's Wellington?"

"He's in the studio right now. He made a significant recovery, and I'm thankful he's well."

"That's great. I need to speak to both of you about an urgent matter, if that is possible. I could be there within the hour."

"He's working on paintings for his next show, but that should not be a problem. I'll tell him you're stopping by."

"I will see you then."

Grace hung up the telephone and walked into Wellington's studio. "Hey, honey. Agent Ramos just called. He wants to talk to us about an urgent matter. He'll be here in an hour."

"Did you tell him I was working? You know it is hard for me to break away." He spoke without turning to look at her.

"Yes, I did. It sounded like the matter could not wait."

"What is 'urgent' is that I finish this painting. You could have checked with me first." He scowled.

"Yeah, you're right. My bad."

"Let me finish a few more strokes before he gets here," he replied, keeping his attention on the painting.

"Sorry about that. I know it's hard for you to stop when you are in a groove." She kissed him on the cheek.

∼

In exactly an hour, Agent Ramos was greeted by Wellington in the hallway.

"You look great man," Ramos told him. "Glad to hear your good-health report."

"Thank you. I am feeling better by the day, thank God. What about you? What have you been up to?" Wellington inquired.

"The usual—tracking down criminals and trying to keep my sanity." Grace offered him a seat. "Would you care for something to drink?"

"No, I'm good. I know you're busy, so I'll get right to the point. There is an elevation of art theft that has come to our attention. An art investment scheme is going on. The FBI and Swiss police are coordinating efforts and ramping up investigation of suspicious developments. The Johansson Gallery is part of the investigation."

"Why are the Johanssons involved?" Grace asked.

"They are one of the top galleries in Geneva that had art stolen from them, and that makes them instrumental in our investigation."

"This has a bad sound to it." Grace produced a disdainful smile.

"If you remember, years ago, when I was working on the art fraud case with Azul, we thought we put a lid on it, but it appears someone has resurrected a global enterprise that is now affecting galleries worldwide."

Wellington sat forward on the couch. "What are your suspicions?"

"The information is inconclusive. I am looking at all sources and trying to see who is heading up the operation. My team is following this closely, but I wanted to bring it to your attention. Ty apparently works closely with the Johanssons."

"You don't think he is involved, do you?"

"I am not sure. But there is interesting history on him that I want to share with you." Agent Ramos went on to explain further.

"Peter Hamilton, Ty's grandfather, started the family's art legacy. He conducted business with Italy's Donato Bonneta, the great art collector, decades ago. Ty's father, Paul Hamilton, was a billionaire and one of the largest art collectors in the world. The family art holdings and assets were passed down to Paul from his father. As a young banker in Zurich, Paul had access to the Swiss vaults where they kept paintings of the European great masters. He gained his wealth doing reproductions of authentic paintings of masters like El Greco, Cézanne, Van Gogh, DaVinci, and Michelangelo. His personal collection was like a museum, with top Renaissance artists. As a young man, Ty did not know the paintings passed down to him were knockoffs, reproduced by his grandfather Peter. The question that stumped Ty was whether his grandfather was part of the situation with Hitler, who realized art was the one commodity that did not depreciate.

"If you recall history, Hitler stole art from England, France, Italy, Poland, and Switzerland. He stole from the Swiss government and hid the paintings in a vault, which eventually was recovered by United States troops. Part of Ty's ambition is to surpass his father's art collection, to be greater than him. The bad blood between Ty and his father, Paul, is because his father always looked down on him. It was no mystery to those in the art circle that Paul felt that Ty, a playboy by most standards, was living off the fat of the land."

"How do you know all of this?" Grace asked.

"It's my job to know. Further, Ty was jealous of his father's collection. It was one of the reasons he was in secret cahoots with Azul to collect art. In his early twenties, Ty and Azul had some troubled deals, and Ty's father, Paul, rescued him. Ty finally cleaned up his act and separated from Azul. I felt giving you background information would help put things in perspective."

"This is the reason why I am anxious to get my product on the expanded market," Grace said.

"In due time, it will happen," Wellington assured her.

"This is not a defining moment. There will be more activity," Agent Ramos announced.

"I just sent some paintings to France. This makes me feel uncomfortable," Wellington said.

"We are looking at different angles and patterns that are emerging. Before you make any more deals, check with me first."

"We will," Grace replied.

"For now, please keep this between us. I will report back as soon as I hear anything."

"Have you shared the information about Ty with Monica?"

"Not yet, but I plan to call her. Remember, your lips are sealed." Agent Ramos put on his worn black hat and left.

Special Agent Carlos Ramos

CHAPTER

21

Hints and Warnings

"This is hard to believe about my fiancée. He told me a little about his past dealings with Azul, but I didn't know his family history with art reproductions," Monica flinched.

"I know this comes as a surprise, but we need to approach him sensibly and with a calm demeanor. Try to keep your emotions out of it. That will be critical. I suggest you ask him some general questions and then give him a chance to respond. Meanwhile, watch yourself," Agent Ramos advised.

"Are you suggesting my life may be in danger?"

"I am asking you to be cautious and stay alert. That is all."

"When I first met Ty, he told me he was through with his old ways, and I believed him. I trusted this man with my entire life and with my friends. I surely don't want my relationship with Wellington and Grace to be compromised because of him." She sighed.

"I don't want you to worry. Like I said, this is still under investigation. We are not jumping the gun on any final conclusions. Do you plan to see him today?"

"Yes. Now that both of us have residences in New York, we have dinner almost every night."

"Good. I need to set up some bugging devices in your home. Can you leave me a key?"

"Yes. I will place it under the rose bush on the left as you enter my place."

"Let me know when you leave, and make sure you bring him back to your house to have a conversation. I want to catch every word he says. We are dealing with a dangerous group of individuals. I hope he's not one of them."

"I appreciate your concern."

"I spoke with Wellington and Grace, and they are aware of this matter. Be cautious of what you say on the telephone."

"I'll call you after dinner to let you know when we are headed to my place."

"You need to be calm and avoid any outright confrontation with him. I will stay in contact with you by telephone," Agent Ramos reminded her.

CHAPTER

22

A Question of Trust

Trust was an important matter for Monica. She felt her relationship with Ty was healthy, but based on Agent Ramos's conversation, things did not add up. She dialed Ty's number, reminding herself of the precarious situation she could very well be in.

"Hey, you. What you up to?"

"Nothing much. I was waiting to hear from you so we can make dinner plans."

"How about meeting at the True Bond Club at five o'clock?"

"I love that place. I will be there."

Monica pulled into the parking lot and reminded herself that no matter what Ty said, she would control her tone and emotions. After the waitress took their order, they made small talk and then enjoyed a delicious dinner. She invited him back to her place and poured him some wine before cunningly starting her questioning.

"I enjoyed dinner tonight. It capped off my day, which was full of new discoveries. Speaking of which, I want to ask you something."

"What's on your mind?" he asked, taking a seat on the couch.

"Remember when we first started dating, and you mentioned that you had some past dealings with Azul?"

"Yes. Why do you ask?" Ty's narrowed his eyes slightly.

"His name came up in a conversation the other day. It was a mess how he died, crashing his car into Wellington's school and bursting into flames. What a way to go. I wish the authorities had caught him instead. That way, he would serve time in jail for all the harm that he did."

"Yes, that was a long time ago, but dying is no small price. He paid handsomely for all he did."

"I guess you're right." Monica changed the subject. "I saw Grace today. She said the new school is awesome, and they are grateful for your financial contributions and support."

"I was happy to help. It was the least I could do after all they have been through."

Monica hesitated before asking the next question. "I also heard the Johansson Gallery might be closing."

"Closing? Why?"

"I'm not totally sure. I know you are close friends. That's why I wondered if you heard anything about that."

"No, I haven't. It comes as a shock to me. What else did Grace say?"

"She mentioned that due to art theft, the gallery suffered heavy financial losses." Monica looked into his eyes for a response.

"I will have to call them and check on them," he said coolly.

"You wouldn't keep anything like this from me, would you?"

"Why would you say that?" he asked.

"You never talk business with me."

"I am not sure what you want me to tell you."

"Anything that I should know."

"I don't know anything about their closing. Right now, I want to enjoy a nice evening with my fiancée without talking business, if that's OK with you," he said, embracing her.

Monica agreed, but she realized that this undoubtedly was a doorway to uncovering more.

That evening Ty was restless and could not sleep. He wondered how much Monica knew and where she was getting her information. He knew he'd now need to be canny to avoid any schism in their relationship.

~

Monica was also restless and could not sleep, so she called Grace.

"Hi, Monica. It's unusual hearing from you this time of night. Are you home or at Ty's place?"

"I'm home. He didn't stay over. It's hard to put a finger on it, but I don't think he's being honest with me about his current business dealings and lifestyle."

"You never mentioned this before. Is this the first time you are feeling this?"

"To be honest, yes. I think I was so infatuated with him that I really wasn't paying attention until Agent Ramos pulled my coat."

"It's concerning to us as well. You know, ever since the creation and talk about LAI, things have changed," Grace mentioned.

"You are probably right. Tonight, when I started asking him some questions, he completely dodged all of them and turned his affection toward me."

"Agent Ramos warned us about some suspicious art matters and said he was going to talk with you. I sure hope they are not true. I wouldn't want to put you in harm's way at all, especially since you are the main one working on this tool."

"This is important to both of us," said Monica. I won't let anything get in our way, not even love."

"Girl, watch what you are saying."

"I mean it!"

"You are my girl, and I wouldn't want anything to disappoint you. This is going to be huge."

"I think we both need to keep our eyes open," Grace cautioned.

"I agree."

"We both knew, coming into this, that trouble might come, and I know God will help us."

"You think it might be a good time to lay low and wait for more information about Ty?"

"That is Agent Ramos's suggestion. He has been right about a lot of things in the past, so I'm going to trust him on this, and I'll pray Ty is clean."

"All right, lady. I got to go. Duty is calling. Talk with you soon."

Ty Hamilton

CHAPTER

23

SoHo Gallery Surprise

It was the second week in May. Grace and Wellington were excited about their combined exhibition at DeeDee's Gallery in the SoHo area of New York City. It was an historic building from the 1800s, wedged between some trendy restaurants and upscale boutiques. An oversized garage door, which was once a horse carriage gateway, marked the entrance into the spacious gallery. Grace, on the cusp of finding commercial success, recently had released several new abstract paintings that were to be unveiled today, alongside Wellington's more surreal and subjective paintings.

Kiko Yamamoto, disguised in a long blonde wig and large round black shades, and wearing a slinky black jumpsuit, entered the gallery and mingled with some of the elite guests. She grabbed a glass of wine and fancy hors d'oeuvres from a gold tray, served by waiters, and continued to scope the entire gallery. She quietly slid out the back door without notice, where her fabulous white stallion awaited. Her goal was to make a spectacular grand entrance. She wanted to send a message. The cadence of the crowd rose with the excitement of people drinking and laughing, while observing Wellington's and Grace's outstanding artwork. Grace was talking with Wellington when Kiko's startling entrance on horseback inside the gallery interrupted them. Her long blonde wig flew wildly as she skillfully maneuvered her white stallion through the crowd toward the center of the room, without knocking over sculptures or upsetting paintings. Her presence was amplified when she picked up one of Wellington's small paintings, placed it under her right arm, and guided the horse through the crowd, all within fifteen seconds, and exited the gallery. The theatrical episode had everyone talking. They didn't know if it was impromptu or part of the exhibition. It was insanity at its highest level. One might say the scene was Lady Godiva-esque. Once outside the gallery—and blocks away—Kiko stepped off her horse and laughed heartily. She had succeeded in stirring up the snobby crowd. She was secretly pleased with her pretentiousness, but more importantly pleased at disrupting Grace's and Wellington's art exhibition.

The next day before the gallery opened, Kinko secretly returned Wellington's painting to its rightful place, which added complexity to the obnoxious episode.

It was fundamentally offensive to Grace. She remembered Kiko from the artist studio party at Owema-A's Gallery and knew she was trying to get into her head. She tried not to focus on Kiko's annoying narcissism but wondered about her ulterior motive.

CHAPTER 24

Olu's Report

Olu Adebayo, a tall businessman from Lagos, Nigeria, was an immaculate dresser, a perfectionist, and was fluent in four languages. He was known as Sergeant. He was wise, but he had a dark side because of an insatiable desire for wealth. His criminal behavior contradicted his culture and upbringing and did not measure up to his professed Pan-African ideology and ancestral teachings.

Kiko Yamamoto, Olu's hot-headed partner in numerous trade operations, was impulsive and always up to something. Her risk-taking often undermined the carefully laid plans of others. He loathed the thought of working with her, but based on the boss's assignment, he had to do so. His inner turmoil, however, led him to call his boss and release his frustrations.

"Hey, it's Sergeant. I'm sure you heard about Kiko's latest escapade."

"No, I haven't. I depend on you to be my eyes and ears."

"Man, no disrespect intended, but Kiko is cynical and undisciplined. She is a loose cannon."

"I think I've heard that one before. What did my granddaughter do this time?"

"She stormed into the middle of a big gallery show on a white stallion and disrupted the atmosphere in the presence of some elite clients."

"When did this happen?"

"Yesterday at DeeDee's Gallery in SoHo, an exhibition featuring the work of Wellington and Grace Holmes."

"Oh, really? The Holmeses? Why on earth is she taking a wrong turn on this assignment? Oh God, that child is interfering with our business. Did you know she is an equestrian?"

"No, but that damn horse belongs on a field, not in a gallery! She constantly drums up dramatic situations," Olu shouted.

"She is quite a peculiar character. I have come to understand she is her own woman. I always hoped that, one day, she would restrain her outrageous thoughts and acts. Most importantly, she needs to stay on course with our mission."

"Man, she is driving me to drink."

"You need to see the big picture. She is talented and clever. And you, my brother, are level-headed and wise. That is why you two make such a good team. You hate to get your hands dirty, but she thinks it's sport and is swift in her ability to eliminate the opposition. She is useful to us."

"Man, I want to choke the living hell out of her."

"I know how you feel."

"Taking risks isn't my forte'. If her quirky behavior continues, I may have to quit the operation," Olu said.

"Let's not jump to any conclusions. I will have a talk with her."

"I'd be grateful to you if you would. Respectfully, please make it sooner rather than later. I don't know how much more I can take of her." Olu ended the call.

Olu Adebayo

Colonel

CHAPTER
25

Japanese Encounter

It had been five years since Wellington's last exhibit in Tokyo. Now, he had received an invitation from Niko Nakamura, curator at the National Art Center.

"Good afternoon, Mr. Holmes." Niko smiled and bowed. "Welcome to our gallery."

"It is good to see you again." Wellington bowed.

"We are excited about your show. Several notable collectors will be attending the event tonight. One of the leading private collectors in Japan has an impressive European collection. He wants you to see his personal collection while you are here."

"Is that right? I am honored."

"Do you have time to visit with him this afternoon before the show?"

"Sure. The show isn't until seven."

"Excellent. I will give him a call."

~

Wellington and Niko Nakamura were greeted by a servant. Then, Itsuki Tanaka, wearing a yukata—a type of informal kimono—met them in the elegantly decorated foyer.

"Welcome, Mr. Holmes." Mr. Tanaka exchanged bows with Wellington.

They entered a room filled with rich tapestries and were served tea as they made light conversation. Itsuki then led the way to the massive room containing his extensive collection.

"Beautiful," Wellington said, walking closer to view the Vermeer, a baroque-period Dutch painting.

"My latest purchase," Itsuki said proudly.

"This is the original?" Wellington asked.

"Yes. I was fortunate to get it."

I swear this original is housed in the Metropolitan Museum in New York, Wellington thought to himself. *Itsuki must be mistaken.*

Knowing the Japanese did not like their shortcomings revealed, Wellington made a mental note to call his friend William Schuster, the curator at the Metropolitan Museum of Art, rather than upset Itsuki. Instead, he said, "May I ask where you purchased this?"

"One of my relatives gave it to me as a gift."

Itsuki continued showing them his collection. Wellington pretended to be interested, but his mind was elsewhere. He thanked Itsuki for the private tour and said that he would see him at the art show later that evening.

Kiko peeked through the sliding door and saw Wellington. She had no idea her uncle had invited him to his house. *Damn!* she thought. *This is not in my plan. This could expose my mission.* She had evil schemes in her heart and needed to be careful at the gallery event or things could go sour for her family, who was unaware of her hidden agenda.

When Wellington arrived at his hotel, he decided to call the Metropolitan Museum of Art, as soon as the museum opens.

~

"Hey, William. How have you been, my friend?" Wellington asked.

"I'm good. Congratulations. I heard you have a big show going on in Tokyo."

"Yes, the show was great. I'm here until tomorrow. I have a matter I want to run past you."

"What is it, my friend?"

"I was invited to a well-known art collector's home yesterday; he has an extensive collection of masters' works. One of his originals stood out like a sore thumb. He has a Vermeer that you have in the museum."

"Which one?" William inquired.

"*Diana and Her Companions.* The thing that disturbed me was that he said it's the original."

"That can't be. It *is* housed here in the museum."

"Wellington said, "You need to make sure. One can never tell, with all the art theft going on."

"I will check and get back with you Wellington. Thanks, man. I appreciate you looking out for us."

"You are welcome."

"By the way, the board reviewed Javier's application and accepted him into our Art Curator program," William said.

"Man, that is awesome! He is going to be so happy. This will help him, before he goes to college, to have an increased career perspective."

"Also, tell Radiance the Matisse exhibit she was looking forward to is coming this fall."

"Thanks for looking out for my family. I'll let them know."

∼

After due diligence, William called Wellington the following day to confirm the original painting was housed in the Metropolitan Museum of Art. "Wellington, the painting you saw has to be a duplicate."

"That's what I thought. Man, I was blown away when I saw it. I hope my face did not give it away. I tried to be cool. I'm going to contact a detective friend of mine at the FBI and alert him to this situation. I'd appreciate you not mentioning or discussing this with anyone until I get back with you. This is a sensitive matter that we should leave to the authorities."

"You have my word. I appreciate your love for the arts."

"Take care. I will talk with you later."

"Congratulations again on your show and keep a keen eye on your originals."

They laughed.

∼

Wellington called Agent Ramos to report his staggering findings.

"Agent Ramos."

"Hey, man. How are you?"

"I'm doing fine. How about you?" Ramos asked.

"I was doing good until yesterday."

"What changed?"

"I am in Tokyo for an art exhibition and came across something startling. I remember you saying that the Swiss government teamed up with the Japanese government on an investigation of reproductions of original art and that crooks were selling them. Man, I believe I had a firsthand experience yesterday."

"Is that right? What happened?" Agent Ramos asked.

"A well-known art collector invited me to his home to show off his impressive personal collection of originals. He has a Vermeer piece, *Diana and Her Companions*, in his collection. He said it was the original, but I know the original is housed at the Metropolitan Museum of Art in New York. I didn't say anything to him. I called my friend William Schuster, the curator at the museum, and he confirmed they have the original. Man, what in the hell is going on in this art world of ours?"

Agent Ramos chuckled. "I am not surprised at all. It's another unidentified case of art fraud."

"You sound so calm about it, but it is alarming to me."

"You have no idea of the level of international crime that is going on right now. I don't know where to begin."

"No, I don't."

"Art reproduction fraud of valuable works of art is a booming business. Real fine art can be more lucrative than currency. It depends on how the stock markets are doing. It is truly global and as old as the history of art itself. In fact, it's the fourth largest criminal enterprise worldwide, grossing six billion dollars a year. These suspected knockoff artists print high-resolution reproductions and pass them off as originals. It is a lucrative business for thieves. It is going on in the States too."

"I had no idea."

"FBI, Scotland Yard, and Italy's carabinieri partnered with my FBI Art Crime team to investigate this matter. The carabinieri have the oldest and largest art theft squad in the world. We have been working on it for a length of time, and this, my friend, is a good lead."

"Man, I don't mean to make more work for you," Wellington said.

"Brother, you are making my job easier right now with this information. I appreciate it. We will investigate this new lead. Meanwhile, don't discuss this with anyone, especially not the collector or anyone else while you are in Tokyo. It's a sore subject for the Japanese. They are proud people who do not like to be looked down on, and they hate to be used. Pretty much like any of us. This information came to the attention of the Japanese government some time ago, and they are aware of it. They hired the team of Aiko Nakama and Saito Tanaka to investigate as well."

"Man, I appreciate what you do. I will stay low key on this. Seems things just keep cropping up."

"You have no idea, my friend. Just enjoy the rest of your trip and be well."

"Thanks, man. Be safe out there."

"Believe me when I say that I always watch my back. I get into more scrapes than you know." Agent Ramos laughed.

~

Agent Ramos put a team together to investigate the various countries and cities where the portrait painters lived. France, Italy, Spain, Tokyo, and New York were on the top of the list. Ramos decided to investigate in Tokyo because he'd heard the famous portrait painter Salvador Franco had a residence there. He remembered that Salvador exhibited with Grace and Wellington in SoHo and hoped that he could identify other portrait painters in the region.

Upon his arrival in Tokyo, a gallery owner told Agent Ramos that many artists hung out in an artsy area in Shimokitazawa, the Bohemian hub, known as the center of subculture in Tokyo. Agent Ramos walked the streets of that area, hoping to gather more information. The atmosphere had a quaint retro vibe, with narrow streets, boutiques, small eateries, chic cafés, theaters, and live music venues. An outside vendor pointed him to a well-known hipster coffee shop where artists typically hung out for lunch.

As Agent Ramos entered the Blikje Button Cafe, he took a seat at the bar, and ordered a coffee. He talked casually with the bartender to inquire about the local artists. The bartender confirmed the café as a place where most of the artists congregated. Agent Ramos returned over the next several days, hoping to see Salvador. After three days, he showed up. On this particular day, he was sitting with a beautiful

Japanese lady, whom Agent Ramos recognized as Kiko. He sat at the bar with his back turned and watched as they laughed and talked intimately. Agent Ramos finished his coffee and left the café with a clear plan in mind.

SEASON 5
Shaping Patterns

CHAPTER 26

Plan Salvador

"Agent Ramos is on the line." Grace handed the telephone to Wellington.

"Hey, man. I told you I would get back to you when I found more information on the artists painting the forgeries. Do you have your phone on speaker so Grace can listen in?"

"Yes."

"I was in Tokyo recently, doing some investigating. I came up with a plan while I was there. But I need your help."

"How can we help?" Wellington asked.

"How would you like to take a vacation to Tokyo?"

"To Tokyo? I cannot just drop what I am doing."

"The agency would cover all costs," Agent Ramos added.

"Wellington, just the other day, you mentioned the seriousness of this matter and that you would help however you could," Grace said. "I am sure Ellona would be willing to take care of Radiance and Javier."

"There you go. It sounds like your family will be taken care of while you are away," Agent Ramos added.

"What is your plan?" Wellington asked.

"You remember Salvador Franco, the portrait artist from Italy who exhibited with you two at Owema-A's Gallery in SoHo?"

"Yes. He told Grace that he wanted to paint her picture." Wellington looked sideways at Grace.

"He asked, but I didn't give him an answer," Grace reminded him.

"Wow, OK, then this would be a perfect time to set up a plan for him to paint your portrait," Agent Ramos said excitedly.

"Paint my portrait?"

"Wait! Where are you going with this?" Wellington asked.

"We are looking for the artists who are painting the replicas, right?" Ramos said.

"Correct."

"Salvador is a famous artist from Italy, and I'm sure he knows several artists. We need a contact who can help us find them."

"How do you know that he will help?" Wellington asked.

"I don't. A light bulb went off in my head, and I got this idea that he might," Ramos added.

"And you want to use Grace to further your light bulb idea Ramos?"

"You haven't heard the whole plan."

"Sounds like you want me and Grace to be like *The Thin Man*."

"No. I am not asking that of you. I am asking that of Grace."

"Man, you have to be kidding. This detective stuff is your line of work, not ours. Besides, it would take us away from the studio," Wellington explained.

"I know, but you haven't heard the entire plan. Just give me a chance to explain. I think it can work. Here is my plan. Every afternoon, Salvador meets his girlfriend, Kiko Yamamoto, at Blikje Button Cafe. I think you'll remember her well. I heard about her unforgettable entrance at your show in SoHo." Agent Ramos chuckled.

"She had a noticeable effect on the entire room. Man, that was the most bizarre moment I ever experienced," Wellington said.

"She is delusional and glamourizes herself," Grace added.

"I have history on her, but that's an issue for another day."

"I cannot wait to hear it," Grace said.

"Anyway, back to my plan. I was led to Blikje Button Café where artists hang out daily. I went in, but I didn't see Salvador. The bartender told me he came in often. I went every day, hoping to see him. One day, he came in. That's when I got the idea. If we play our cards right, this could be an opportunity to request that he paint Grace's portrait. Then Grace can inquire about buying art. This could lead to information about the replicas. You never know."

"Agent Ramos, you are always coming up with something, but why include us in this outrageous plan?" Wellington asked.

"Keep your mind open. All of this can end up protecting your family. We could plan a disturbing scene in the café between you and Grace to get Salvador's attention. I won't put you in harm's way without a backup. You know how artists love beautiful women. This is where Graces comes in. Grace, you and Wellington have a minor argument, and Wellington will storm out of the café. When Salvador sees Grace, his head will turn, and she will get his attention. That will be Grace's opportunity to inquire about buying art."

"I am not so sure I like this plan," Grace said. "I haven't sat for anyone besides Wellington."

"It is not a good idea!" Wellington interrupted.

"Think about it before you say no," Agent Ramos said.

"I'm doing my best to follow what you are saying," Grace said.

"What makes you think I want somebody to paint my wife? Why should I dangle her out there like a carrot? She is my woman, and I don't like the thought!"

"I think I detect a little jealousy from Wellington," Grace said.

"You always paint beautiful women, and I am cool about it, even when they have other intentions."

"That's different. That's what I do!"

"Oh, I see." She smiled. "The shoe is on the other foot for the art-loving husband." She laughed.

"It ain't like that."

"I think it's a good idea to try to extract information from Salvador. Besides, you know our goal," Grace said.

"I thought you were an artist, not a detective," Wellington snapped.

"I never wanted to be a detective, but I have some interesting past experiences. There was a level of suspense that was exciting, even when I didn't know how everything would end."

"Stop bragging, woman. That was the grace of God that helped you through those situations. Besides, it is not just the danger that concerns me. I know how artists think."

"Now, now, you two. Stop the quarreling," Agent Ramos said. "Salvador is accustomed to painting many beautiful tourists, so this would not be out of the norm. It's worth trying something out of the box."

"I know how this works because I see it through an artist's eye," Wellington said.

"Oh? And what does that look like?" Grace asked.

Wellington started to stammer, but Grace cut him off.

"Yes, just what I thought. I will do what I can to help in the name of justice and perhaps learn more firsthand about forgery in the art world," Grace said.

"If I could quote Shakespeare from *A Midnight Summer's Dream*— 'Though she be but little, she is fierce!'" Agent Ramos laughed.

"Stay out of this!" Wellington retorted. "This could still be risky."

"Nah, I don't believe so. We just want to find out what Salvador knows. When people are distracted and their attention is on something else, they reveal more than they need to," Agent Ramos said.

"Yes. Distracted by lust. That's what I am talking about."

"Now, let's stay focused on our intent. I believe if we follow him, it will bring us to the mastermind behind this operation. Are you willing to give it a try?"

"Let me think about it," Wellington said hesitantly. "If we choose to help, what then?"

"If you choose *not* to is what concerns me more."

"I'm not down with this. We are going to pass on this scheme right now," Wellington said.

Grace was quiet, thinking that she wanted to help Monica, who was in a precarious position with her fiancé.

"It is an opportunity, if you are interested; that's all. Take a few days to think about it."

"There you go, trying to set my schedule for me again," Wellington said.

"I'm just saying, man—it's a concrete plan that could work. Call me," Agent Ramos said before hanging up the telephone.

CHAPTER 27

Blikje Button Cafe

After talking things over with Grace and hearing her concerns about Dr. Monica and Ty, and considering her risk as an essential part in the development of LAI, Wellington relented and agreed to the trip to Tokyo. He shook his head in amazement as he thought about the velvety skills Grace had used to persuade him to see things in a different light.

Prior to leaving for Tokyo, Agent Ramos informed Wellington and Grace about the type of replicas sold on the market. Grace looked like a tourist, wearing jeans, an oversized blouse, sporty designer walking shoes, and designer sunglasses. When she entered Blikje Button Café, she noticed Salvador sitting alone near a window. As she passed him, she added an extra sway in her walk, just as Ellona would. She approached the table in the corner, where Wellington sat with his back facing the bar. They started their "argument," and Wellington raised his voice for all to hear.

"I told you not to buy that expensive painting," he yelled, adding a few expletives. He stood up and stormed out of the café.

Just as planned, Grace lowered her head and walked slowly to the bar, getting Salvador's full attention.

After a few moments, he walked over and stood next to her, observing her beauty. Enticed by her alluring scent, he said, "Aren't you Grace Holmes, the artist?"

"Yes," she said without looking up.

"I'm Salvador. We exhibited together at Owema-A's Gallery in Soho."

Grace looked up and focused on his face. "Oh yeah. I remember you. I'm sorry. My mind was on something else."

"Is everything all right?"

"It will be. I had an argument with my husband over some paintings." She pouted.

"Anything I can do to help?"

"He is upset because I want to buy more paintings. He will get over it."

"Excuse my concern. Do you mind if I sit down?"

"Sure." She pointed to the barstool next to her.

"Would you like a drink?"

"No, thanks. I don't know how I am going to get through this," Grace said exaggerating her distress by rubbing her forehead.

"Through what?" he inquired.

"I still need to buy more paintings for my client."

"Maybe I can be of assistance."

"You? Aren't you a portrait painter?" she said, looking up at him.

"Yes."

"Ah, you probably could not help me, then. I'm looking for the old masters' paintings."

"Maybe I can help. Perhaps we can talk about it while I paint your beautiful face. You know I asked you that question the last time I saw you."

"Paint me? I don't understand why you want to do that," she said shyly.

"You have a beautiful neckline that I would love to capture."

"Oh, I get it. It is a tradeoff." She smiled.

"Maybe we can work something out. I am available tomorrow. Could you come to my studio here in Tokyo?" he asked, handing her his card.

"I see you work quickly."

"I am just trying to help out a pretty lady."

"I am leaving for New York in a few days so that would put a tight squeeze in my schedule."

"Sounds like getting more paintings is of more importance to you, right?"

"Yes, it is."

"This is Asia. I can easily get my hands on a few paintings that you can look at."

"Really? You would do that? But what about my portrait? How can you do all of that in a short time?"

"Capturing your beauty may take longer, but I am good at working miracles when it comes to paintings. I will see you tomorrow?" he asked.

"Sounds like you have this all worked out. Is this your MO with all the ladies?" She produced a questionable smile.

"No. Only the subject before me right now." He smiled.

"What time?"

"Noon?"

"I might be able to fit that in my schedule, but I need to be clear on something first."

"What is that?"

"I don't do nudes!" Grace said emphatically.

"Ah. That's too bad. I'd bet you have a lovely body," he said, sizing her up.

"As I said, I don't do nudes!"

"That's not a problem. I will see you tomorrow?"

"I'll be there at noon."

Kiko Yamamoto entered the café and saw the two smiling at each other as Grace got up from the bar stool.

Grace noted Kiko's flawless skin and shapely body and purposely avoided direct eye contact as she left the café.

"You are at it again, I see," Kiko said as she approached Salvador. "Always wooing the pretty ladies."

"That's Grace Holmes, the artist I exhibited with in New York."

"I know who she is! I was in New York too, remember?"

"She was quarreling with her husband over money and paintings. Lucky for us—it looks like we may have a new customer."

"We will see about that! Looks and luck can be deceiving." Kiko glared at him.

"It is not your business."

"I can make it my business," Kiko snapped.

"Always the jealous one," he said, touching her cheek. "She is a future client. Just let me do what I do, and don't interfere."

"Always the bossy one," she retorted and turned her head when he attempted to kiss her.

CHAPTER

28

A Daunting Task

Salvador's studio was a converted factory, located on a side street lined with multiple buildings that were revamped into stylish lofts. Grace was not surprised to see the spacious workspace. To her, it held a hint of mystique, romance, and adventure, with its modest furniture and large windows that allowed ample light to flow in. The space had separate rooms with closed doors. Easels, turpentine-steeped rags, and empty alcohol bottles lined the floor, but there was a clear uncluttered working space in the center, containing a large blank canvas.

Grace was more on edge than she'd expected. Salvador greeted her with a warm smile and handed her a purple drape to fit over her right shoulder. Grace wore a crisp white button-down shirt, strapless bra, and a soft blue linen skirt. With an incredulous look, and trepidation, she took a seat and held her trembling hands close to her side.

"Just relax," he advised. "You looked strikingly beautiful."

"Are you sure this is the position you want me to hold?" she asked.

He drew nearer, touched her chin softly, cupped her face in his hand, and repositioned her.

She noticed the small scar on his otherwise unblemished right cheek.

"Keep your chin pointed up," he said.

Grace stopped breathing. She felt varying degrees of unspoken emotion.

"The more still you are, the better the portrait will be."

The cadence of his voice was soothing, yet it still exasperated her. Although Grace had sat for Wellington many times in his studio, this sitting was uncomfortable, simply because of the way Salvador looked at her. She was tense and worried. The classical music playing in the background helped to slowly ease her tightness. She tried not to see his almond eyes, high cheek bones, and unevenly shaved facial hair. Instead, she went inside her mind to find the right questions to ask about purchasing artwork, hoping to identify more portrait painters in the area. The session lasted several hours before she was able to breathe easily. She stood to stretch and asked the direction to his restroom, as he excused himself to make a telephone call.

On her way to the restroom, she noticed a room with a door that was slightly cracked open. Checking on his whereabouts first, she pushed it open farther. Sitting in the corner was one of Wellington's old paintings. She gasped and quickly exited the room and entered the restroom to regain her composure.

Within a given time, she returned to the studio before Salvador came back into the room.

Noticing that her face looked pallid, he asked, "Are you OK?"

Grace lied. "I have to admit I peeked at my portrait. You caught me. You produced an impressive true likeness." She smiled.

"Do you like it?"

"I cannot believe it's me. It is beautiful."

"Then it is a true likeness." He beamed. "I will put the final touches on it tomorrow, which should take only a few hours."

After she left, Salvador fantasied about her enticing neckline, long beautiful legs, and captivating brown eyes. He had painted many women in his lifetime but none that left him as spellbound as Grace. He knew he could not let Kiko see the portrait, or her uncontainable suspicions would explode.

Grace's spirit was troubled. As a wife and mother and as a virtuous woman, she had to be careful and not fall into any carnal traps. After all, she was human, too. This new territory called for maintaining a moral compass, just as she had told her daughter.

That evening, Wellington was unusually quiet, which she summed up as his annoyance at her sitting for another artist. The tension between them that evening was intense.

~

The next day, Salvador drew his brush in an upswept motion, signaling completion, as he put the final touch on Grace's portrait. He sprayed it with a finisher and set it aside to dry.

"We haven't spoken about the paintings that I want to buy. I thought you were going to show me something before I leave," Grace reminded him.

"I haven't forgotten. I have a few to show you. Give me a moment, and I will bring them out." He left the room and returned with four small originals.

He showed her a Matisse and a few other artists Grace knew.

Grace pretended to be interested as she examined each closely. "My client is very particular. Do you mind if I take pictures of these?"

Grace sensed his hesitancy, even though he said, "Sure. Anything for the pretty lady."

She took several pictures with her cell phone and wrote down the prices.

"When I return to New York, I will be in touch with you to let you know my client's decision."

"I can make these available any time you are ready. Once your portrait dries, I will make sure I get it to you. It was a pleasure to have you sit for me."

"Thank you. It turned out better than I thought. Should I expect to receive it within two weeks?"

"I will do better than that. I will deliver it in person."

"That would be nice of you. Maybe I can see more originals at that time."

"I can arrange that."

"Great. Are there other portrait artists in this region as good as you?"

"There are a few but none as good as me. I am much like Picasso," he bragged. "He was a genius at age fifteen. His work was so dynamic at a young age that he could duplicate the masters' works."

Grace pondered his last words. She was thankful she was wearing a wire, to catch that important message. She could not wait to leave.

"I look forward to seeing you again soon," he said, touching her lightly on the arm.

Grace felt uncomfortable about that touch. Something within her spirit signaled trouble. She wondered how she got herself into this, and then she reminded herself again that Dr. Monica's life had become compromised, based on the creation of the LAI tool, and they were looking for ways to uncover the truth about the art thefts. Determined to control her discomfort, Grace smoothly stepped away from Salvador and headed back to her hotel. Once inside her room, she exhaled with relief, then thought about her family. She called Ellona to make sure all was well.

"Hey, girl, how's everything?"

"I should be asking you that, world traveler," Ellona said. "Are you having fun?"

"Trying to, but this trip is just a little different. How are Javier and Radiance?"

"Everyone is fine. Javier is enjoying his new job at the museum, and Radiance, as always, is studying and painting."

"That's good. I needed to hear your voice for reassurance and comfort."

"Your mom called the other day and spoke with Radiance. Whatever she said left a big smile on Radiance's face, and she's been in a joyful mood ever since."

"That's good to hear. I'm so blessed to have both of you in her corner. Tell everyone we will see them in a couple days."

"OK, girl. Be safe, and we will talk when you get back."

CHAPTER
29

Shadow of Doubt

Grace and Wellington handed their tickets to the Delta Airlines flight attendant for the twelve plus hours flight back to New York. Grace felt eyes were on her and glanced over her shoulder to see a Japanese female in dark clothes and dark shades standing near a wall. She knew it was not her imagination—Kiko, with a smirk on her face, was following her.

Kiko's thoughts were racing with skepticism. As a *shihan*, an honorific title for a Japanese martial arts expert, she was not a rival you would want to meet in a dark alley.

"I would be careful if I were you. The last model Salvador painted did not fare so well," Kiko snickered to herself.

That following Sunday morning, Wellington and Grace were having breakfast in a New York café, when a text message appeared on Grace's phone. It was from Salvador.

"Is he texting you again?" Wellington asked.

"Yes. He will be in New York in two weeks and will set up a meeting to see more paintings. I'll let Agent Ramos know."

"Are you sure he is not coming just to see you?"

"Wellington, there you go again. I told you many times—no. Our goal is to discover the artist who's drawing the replicas. When I saw a replica of your original in his house, it was a confirmation that he is up to something. We just need to dig deeper and find out what that is."

"I still wonder why you took a chance in sneaking around in his place like that. He could have caught you."

"I was not going to let that happen. I knew where he was. I tried to do a little spying—that's all."

"You never talked about the sitting. I am curious how it went. Was he flirtatious?"

"No. He did his job and painted a nice portrait. You will see it."

"Are you prepared to be introduced to his art distributor?"

"I am a little nervous," she admitted. "Agent Ramos has designated someone from his team to handle that meeting."

"I feel better about it already. This is probably getting to both of us. We will need a real vacation after this is over."

"Yes. But for now, we have unfinished business to take care of," Grace said.

～

Grace needed to download some of her feelings and decided to call Ellona.

"Can we talk?"

"What is going on, Mrs. International Traveler?"

"It isn't as much fun as it sounds. I have to tell you something that I'm not supposed to tell, but it's eating away at me. I definitely cannot tell my mom yet."

"Then it must be big. You tell her almost everything."

"You must promise to keep this between us. My life depends on it."

"Girl Scouts honor." Ellona placed her hand across her heart.

"You know how I feel about art and the criminals who are dangerously ripping people off. I am in deep!" Grace explained the scenario in Tokyo and then said, "Wellington thinks what I am doing is nonsense. I think I may have stuck my neck out too far."

"Sounds like you are speaking from fear or panic," Ellona said.

"Probably both," Grace acknowledged. "Salvador is different."

"Why don't you let me help you? We can work as a team. You know how I love excitement, and besides, Italian men are sexy."

"I cannot keep getting you involved in my drama. Last time a handsome man was involved, you almost got us killed," Grace said.

"Yes, that was scary, but I learned my lesson. Like I told you before, you do not know these street gangsters like I do. They are out of your league. You need someone like me to help you navigate all of this. Your drama is my drama, girlfriend. Besides, I cannot let you have all the fun. Let's work out a plan. You know how we do it. You cannot diss me. I am your angel in disguise," Ellona reminded her.

"It is such a dangerous time in our business," Grace acknowledged with sadness.

"With all we've been through, you know I got your back."

"I know; that's why I need you to keep this to yourself."

"No worries. I got you, girl."

"There is more. Salvador's girlfriend, Kiko, eyed me when we were in Tokyo. She looked at me in the strangest way. Why would she do that?"

"Probably jealous of you."

"Kiko doesn't have any reason to be jealous of me," Grace said.

"Oh, but you are wrong, my dear. Have you taken a good look in the mirror lately? Apparently, your beauty is a threat to her."

"This girl is pretty, but she has an evil presence."

"Isn't she the one who stormed into the SoHo art show on a white stallion?"

"Yes. She is a piece of work. I might need help with her."

"Angel in disguise at your service," Ellona said. "I've been up against a few jealous females before."

"She's got some juju going on."

"She can bring all the evil she wants, but she has no authority over us. That's what's up!"

"You are so street, child." Grace laughed.

"I swear, if she brings it, she will have a fight on her hands, messing with my girl."

Grace laughed again. "I needed to get this stuff off my chest. This is a special operation with Agent Ramos so I cannot disclose any more. As it develops, I will keep you informed. Thanks for listening. I will call you if I need you."

"Girl, call me!"

CHAPTER 30

My Way or No Way

"You have remarkable raw talent, and I'm not speaking of painting," Kiko said.

"What are you talking about, woman?" Salvador inquired.

"Your way with women. You are not fooling me," Kiko said.

"What nonsense are you talking again? Fooling you about what?"

"Your friend Grace. You are going to New York to see her. All you have to do is mail her the portrait."

"You need to put your feelings in check."

"You never traveled anywhere to see me. Am I as relevant as Grace?"

"Do I sense a hint of jealousy," he asked, kissing her on the neck. She pushed him away.

"You seem to forget the mission of selling her paintings. That's why I am going."

"I don't understand why she wants to buy art from you. She can buy them from anyone."

"She has a client who wants prominent paintings from the masters—that's it."

"I know women. She has another motive."

"Do you want me to mail the portrait? Will that settle your little mind since you cannot seem to trust me?"

"Yes. Do it! Set her up with Olu, our New York contact. That will not be a problem, will it?" Kiko huffed.

"If it puts you at ease, I will do it. Are you happy now?" he asked, kissing her softly. Kiko produced a wry smile, but he did not recognize the slickness in her eyes.

"If you weren't so charming, I would kill you," she said playfully.

To please Kiko, Salvador mailed the portrait and called Grace to provide the New York contact's number, which spoiled all chances of his seeing her.

Kiko was an arrogant and self-absorbed person. She had a separate agenda from Salvador's amorous agenda. By anyone's standard, she was a strikingly beautiful woman, but she was insecure and suspicious of Salvador's female clients. While he was asleep, she checked his phone and saw several pictures of Grace, which infuriated her and enveloped her in evil imaginings. Her love for him was not without reprisal.

CHAPTER 31

The Pierre Hotel, New York

Olu Adebayo, that astute businessman who dealt in international art trading, possessed the flair of an entertainer but, at the same time he was intimidating. As a curator, he had a clean reputation—up until eight years ago, when he met a man who offered financial rewards for an early retirement. It was a dream come true to return to Nigeria, richer than most wealthy and successful people.

Olu had attended the University of Oxford in Cambridge, England. He earned a degree in art history and received a Master of Fine Art at Oxford's Ruskin School. He had been a curator at the Museum of Egyptian Antiquities in Cairo years ago. Four years ago, he became the curator of the Metropolitan Museum of Art in New York. Known in elite art circles as a valued member of the Metropolitan Art Board of Trustees, he was highly respected for raising millions of dollars for the museum. It gave Olu leverage to select works that the museum purchased.

In a surprise move, he resigned from his position, and William Schuster stepped into the role of curator. Only a few knew Olu's motive was a calculated move for the future.

Lillian Sanders, a member of Agent Ramos's FBI Art Crime team was chosen as Grace's client who would meet with Olu to inquire about paintings. She checked her wire and then stepped in front of the mirror and applied the final touches to her makeup. She adjusted her navy-blue suit and curly red wig and was pleased that the combination complemented her rosy complexion. She grabbed her purse and put on her dark sunglasses before stepping out the door.

The Pierre Hotel of New York, a symbol of elegance, class, and luxury, was chosen as their meeting place. It was a quintessential landmark in New York City, located on the doorstep of Central Park. Olu looked around the suite to ensure all was in place before having his assistant answer the door for his new client.

Olu was an imposing picture of elegance and grace when he greeted Lillian at the door. They walked through a spacious hallway which led to a large room with an assortment of luxurious items. Lillian took note of everything. The crystal chandelier suspended from the ceiling made a dramatic statement. Expensive Persian silk rugs lined the floor. The room was adorned with the masters' paintings on easels and artifacts on tables. Luxurious tasteful cream-colored furniture was placed throughout the sizeable room.

With a broad knowledge of art, Lillian effortlessly engaged in intellectual conversation and skillfully answered Olu's questions. After studying several paintings, she selected a medium-sized painting and paid him with marked money provided by the agency.

Olu's assistant wrapped the item; Olu and Lillian exchanged business cards and shook hands, and she departed. Shortly after she left, a knock came at the door. Olu thought it was Lillian, returning for more. To his surprise, two men flashed FBI badges in his face.

"Olu Adebayo?"

"That's me."

"We are taking you down for questioning."

"For what?"

"We are investigating your involvement in suspicious art activity. Come with us. You have the right to remain silent. Anything you say can be used against you in court," the officer said as he grabbed Olu's arms and handcuffed him.

"I want to call my lawyer."

"You will get your opportunity." The officer pushed him into the elevator.

∼

Later that evening, Agent Ramos met with Lillian to examine the painting. He shook his head in disbelief.

"I wouldn't know if this is a replica or the original." He held it to the light. "It looks like the real thing! This is exactly the evidence we need." He smiled.

"How will we know if it is a replica?"

"There are markings that make the difference. Our crosscheck and confirmation will come from the museum. When Grace's LAI product went on the market, several museums placed the LAI tool on the back of their originals. My job is to find out who owns the original—a museum or a private owner. This is a good test to see how we should proceed to track down the abusers."

"I sensed this is a sophisticated operation with a mastermind involved," Lillian said.

"No doubt. Olu is smart enough not to show all the cards in his hand."

"There is something about him that makes me nervous around him."

"To all that, you say what?" Agent Ramos asked.

"Things went almost too perfectly. He appeared overly confident and slightly arrogant."

"That is the nature of criminals. Salvador directed us to him, but I think Salvador is a pawn in this operation, which begs me to ask—who are the artists painting the reproductions?" Ramos mused aloud.

"We will find out," Lillian said.

"Well done, Lillian. I have faith that it will all come together. By now, the FBI agents have picked up Olu for questioning. They will detain him for a short time and see what information he will divulge. It is a scare tactic that we hope will work."

CHAPTER

32

Eye Matters

After enjoying a relaxing treatment at Spa 52, Grace left and walked to her car. As she opened the door to her Mercedes, Kiko stepped out of the shadows and blocked her from entering her vehicle. They stood eye to eye. Grace could not believe how Kiko crept up at the most dubious times. Her demeanor was unsettling. On top of that, in her crossed arms she was holding drumsticks. That was odd to Grace, who had no idea of the meaning of the sticks.

"Why are you bothering my man?" Kiko demanded.

"Excuse me! Bothering your man? Girl, please." Grace laughed. "He's cute and talented, but I have a husband."

"Don't play dumb. I see how Salvador looks at you." Kiko produced a distasteful look.

"Girl, you are plain crazy. My connection with him is strictly business. You should know that."

"Why does he mention your name all the time? Something must be up."

"What is *up* is your paranoia," Grace said emphatically.

"Paranoia about what?"

"You tell me. You are the one questioning me," Grace replied, unmoved by Kiko's scowl.

"You make me want to throw up, with your false virtue and humility. I see right through you." Kiko glared at her.

"I am not sure about your x-ray vision, but a wise man once said, 'Humility is the solid foundation of all virtues.' You might want to take some lessons."

Kiko, her face full of rage, switched gears. "Give me that LAI," she demanded. "I want it now!"

"Oh! Is that what this is all about?" Grace laughed.

"You are trying to interrupt a lucrative business, and I won't let that happen on my watch."

"All right, then. Here it is—L. A. Eye," Grace said. She reached down in her purse with her free hand, pulled out the LAI sample, and sprayed directly in Kiko's face. Grace remembered Dr. Monica telling her that the chemical used to create the formula for LAI was a major skin and eye irritant. If sprayed in the eyes, it would affect the cornea, causing uncontrollable tearing, redness, swelling, stinging, closing of the eyelids, and temporary blindness.

Disoriented by the spray, Kiko rubbed her eyes, which increased the intensity of pain. She bent backward in agony. "I am warning you to watch your step, やりま [slut]," she said, pointing toward Grace.

Grace knew Kiko had uttered something hostile that she could not understand. By now, Grace's amiable nature had disappeared, and she blurted a response as she walked around Kiko, keeping her distance. "Don't underestimate me, Miss Thang. This ain't my first rodeo." Grace slammed her car door and sped away.

Grace refused to be distracted or let anyone hijack her

mission. She could and would hold her own—even against this eccentric woman.

～

As soon as Grace was out of Kiko's sight, she pulled over. She stared at her phone a long time before dialing Agent Ramos.

"Grace. You sound winded. What is going on?"

"This is becoming dangerous," she said, her breathing uneven. "I don't understand why she keeps following me."

"What is becoming dangerous, and who is following you? Slow down and tell me what is going on."

"Kiko is following me. She is in New York and cornered me when I came out of Spa 52, and then she threatened me. Something is definitely lacking in her nature."

"What did she say?"

"She told me to leave her man alone, and she wanted the formula."

"The formula? Ah ha! What did you tell her?"

"Well, I was not so nice. I said OK, and then I sprayed the LAI in her face."

"Grace? You didn't!"

"Yes, and I am not proud that I participated in an ugly exchange of words, but I needed to come to my own defense. I am not scared of her," she said boldly, although her insides were trembling.

"You been hanging with me too long. I am beginning to rub off on you." He laughed.

"That is a good thing if I am going to be dealing with peculiar people like her. The frequency of her exploits is getting on my nerves. I feel like I am walking on eggshells with her," Grace lamented.

"Grace, you are a resilient woman. Nobody can stop you on this mission. She is a mere facsimile of the demons you fought off in the past."

"But where is God in all of this?" Grace asked.

"Believe me, God will do what is necessary through you. It is all in Grace's seasons. Our lives are a book of seasons, and life itself teaches us many things. Your intentions are to bring justice, and that takes courage and patience; it takes time. You told me once that spiritual power is more powerful than evil."

"Yes, I remember that."

"Remember, then, that you are a warrior. We will find a way to keep her at a distance."

"Somebody better. If she continues to push me, I cannot promise that the real warrior woman in me won't show up."

Agent Ramos chuckled. "I did my own investigation on Kiko and heard some atrocious stories, but you may not want to hear them."

"Didn't you just tell me not to fear?"

"Yes, I did."

"Then let me hear and judge for myself."

"OK. Remember—you asked. Here is some background on her. Kiko is an international model by day and a jazz drummer by night."

"Oh, she is an artist?"

"Yes. She sits in on jazz sessions at various clubs. She played with top jazz groups like Hiroshima, Boney James, McCoy Tyner, Journey—and once, she sat in with Wynton Marsalis. She is also a master at martial arts, and she always carries her drumsticks with her. It is said she uses them as a weapon. One time, while she was playing in New York, a belligerent drunk came up to her, and she stuck him in the eye with one stick and hit him in his lower extremities with the other. They dragged him out the club, and she kept on playing. On another occasion, while she was in Philly, a guy had a knife, and she took one stick, and poked him in the eye and drove the knife into his knee."

"*Stop!* I don't need to hear any more. When she approached me at my car, she had those drumsticks in her hands. I am sure she was trying to bully me or scare me. I get it! She is vicious, and that is the secret of her charm. I am sure now that I have to warrior up," Grace announced.

∼

The stories Agent Ramos told about Kiko left Grace with an empty feeling. Torn and wrestling with racing thoughts, Grace's antidote in moments like these were to call her mom for counsel and encouragement.

"Sounds like you are in a battle," Ruth said after hearing Grace's story.

"That's putting it mildly." Grace grimaced.

"It appears you are facing a giant, like David did with Goliath. Do you know that when you are in a battle, the angels excel in strength? That is found in Psalm 103:20. The most important thing to remember is that God is on your side."

"Mom, that's a good word. I needed that encouragement. I believe I am also in conflict with myself."

"Have you asked yourself why?"

"Why do you say that?"

"It is important to have honest conversations with yourself—a self-assessment to get to the bottom of an internal issue. You knew when you designed the LAI that the road would not be easy. It never is when you stand up for something that is right."

"Yes, Mom."

"Nothing is going to come easy. You will have trouble, but you must push through. That is what a friend of mine told me. She reminded me of the words of that song, 'It is my destiny and too important to give up for anything.' I know you've heard it before."

"Yes, I love that song. You are right. Thanks for your advice and for your calming effect."

"Remember, God fights the battle for you. Trust him. But you also must stay alert. I believe you are doing a good job and I am proud of you. Remember Proverbs 2:7—'Let God be your shield.'"

SEASON 6
Unfathomable Disclosures

CHAPTER 33

Informant Disclosure

After months of trying to crack open the rampant art-theft cases, Agent Ramos received a tip from an eager informant who wanted to lessen his jail time. It was a dramatic story, and Agent Ramos didn't know which part to believe.

"I swear on my mother's grave—I am not lying."
"What are you looking to get out of this?" Agent Ramos asked.
"I want less jail time."
"What makes you think I'll believe you? You lied before, so why are you bothering me with this nonsense? Don't you know I am a busy man?"
"It is not safe in here, and I have come to grips with telling the truth. I knew if anyone would listen to me, it would be you."

"What makes you think this is the guy I'm looking for?"

The informant shared information he heard through prison gossip about an infamous and elusive criminal involved in many art schemes. He did not have a name, but the man had ties with many countries, including Russia, Switzerland, Japan, and Poland. The man was slippery and managed to evade all law officials. He had extraordinary style and an appearance of luxury. He gained allies but also accumulated many enemies. He was an avid gambler, and he fixed horse races.

The informant also told Agent Ramos a story about a conspired horse theft. A millionaire client in Monte Carlo had commissioned the man to paint a portrait of the client's ten horses—he had a slew of winning racehorses. The criminal hired a portrait painter from Italy. When the horses were to be removed from his stable for the sitting, they were missing. The client lost millions of dollars.

"I don't know what went down," the informant said, "but the criminal craftily sold them back to the owner under a disguise. It sounds like embezzlement and that the criminal had some dirt on the client. The police were never involved. The client paid him twenty million dollars to get the horses back. The criminal successfully bamboozled him."

"Do you have information on where he is right now?"

"They say he has a villa in Monte Carlo, but he has several residences all over the world."

"Where did you hear that?"

"It's the word on the yard."

"Do you know what he looks like?"

"Not from here. That's your work, Agent Ramos."

"If I were you, I would not be getting smart right now. I think your life depends on this. Besides, why should I believe you?"

"Man, I am telling you the truth." He wiped the perspiration from his forehead. "He's also known to have deals in Turkey."

"What kind of deals?"

"They say he formed an alliance with this guy named Pascual

who was handpicked as one of the best schemers in pulling off scams. They renovated a mansion and turned it into an art gallery. Wealthy people from Turkey and Greece were invited to a party, where they introduced and sold original paintings of Ethiopian women."

"Who are you talking about? Pascual or the criminal?"

"The criminal set it up. Pascual was the middle guy. Many buyers purchased what they thought were originals, but they were reproductions. They were told they were painted by a famous artist. Word on the street is the man and Pascual closed shop, and nobody heard from them again."

Agent Ramos had heard enough. "Lock him back up, Officer." Agent Ramos then turned to the informant. "Your stories are questionable, to say the least. I need to check them out before I'll think about lightening your sentence. Until then, you will stay in prison."

"You lied to me!" the informant shouted as the officer pulled him away. "You promised parole! I promise you will regret this!"

Agent Ramos turned over questions in his head. This startling new clue prompted him to book a trip to Monte Carlo to find out if the information was real or a fabricated story.

CHAPTER

34

Window of Opportunity

Agent Ramos waited for his boss, Amare Jackson, head of the National Security branch of the FBI Art Crime team, to get off the phone before entering his office. With thirty years of experience, Jackson was no-nonsense and strict about abiding by the rules, which Agent Ramos sometimes bent.

"What you got, Ramos?" Jackson asked.

"A tip from an informant that could lead to information on the art theft cases."

"Oh yeah?" he replied, preoccupied with paperwork.

"An informant at Rikers asked to see me. He wanted to give up information in exchange for a shorter sentence."

"That's nothing new. What did he say?"

"He said there was an infamous crime kingpin with different enterprises, and there may be a link to art," Ramos said.

"Somebody must have rubbed him the wrong way in prison; otherwise, he would not be talking."

"Well, I listened, and some of what he said aroused my curiosity."

"What do you want from me?" Jackson asked.

"I have been working night and day, and I need a break. I want a few days of vacation to think this through."

"Ramos, you are not gonna be relaxing. I know good and well something's up. What is it?"

"I got a hunch, Boss, that this may be vital information for our case."

"What is so different about this?"

"The same ole' thing—the mastermind behind the art-theft operations. I feel I'm getting closer."

"It is teamwork, Ramos. Get that through your thick skull. You cannot keep venturing out on your own. That is where you get in trouble. Next thing you know, my boss will be calling and saying you messed up again. I don't want to wake up in the middle of the night in a cold sweat over dead bodies."

"Boss, working alone has been my MO for so many years. It is hard to break. I am working on it, Boss."

"Work harder on this, man, because you have no reason to work alone. There is no *I* in *team*."

"You forget that I think like these criminals. My records reflect that—by the number of individuals we put in prison."

"Ramos, there's no room in this business for patting yourself on the back. Like I said, work harder, and learn to enjoy that we all work together to accomplish the same goal."

"I get it. We *all* are fighting an invisible enemy. So what about that vacation? I am due for it."

"Where are you going?"

"To Monte Carlo."

"Now, that's a vacation! I know you got more up your sleeve but take a couple of weeks. Now get out of my office—and you better stay out of trouble."

"Thanks, Boss."

Amare Jackson

CHAPTER 35

Grand Hotel Tremezzo

Agent Ramos considered Amare Jackson's advice and changed his original plan from checking out the informant's information to getting some "me-time" first. Northern Italy was the ideal spot for a real vacation. The Grand Hotel Tremezzo on Lake Como, Italy, was known for its natural beauty and handsome villas, where aristocrats and celebrities lived and took vacations. The upscale resort was located at the foothills of the Alps. Its luscious green scenery was an ideal backdrop for spa treatments and fine dining. At two o'clock that afternoon, Agent Ramos strode through the lobby, checking out the pretty women and flirting as they strutted past him in bathing suits, stilettos, and flimsy garments.

With a book in hand, he stepped onto the pool patio and chose a table in the corner, where he could get a panoramic view of the vivid blue water. He ordered a margarita. The familiar aroma of a cigar hit his nose, causing him to turn around. He saw a man with salt-and-pepper hair, who seemed to be a gentleman. He had a close-shaved beard and appeared to be in his forties. He was seated with a beautiful Japanese woman in a skimpy pink bathing suit and sun hat. They appeared comfortable and familiar with each other.

Agent Ramos's interest was piqued when he recognized the lady as Kiko. He took quick peeks at them while reading his book. Something about the man was familiar, but he could not put his finger on it. He continued reading his book. It was not until the couple got up to leave that Ramos's inquisitive nature took over.

The man grabbed his cane, put his cigar into the ashtray, and walked away with a familiar limp. Agent Ramos shook his head. Maybe his eyes were playing tricks on him. An alarm went off in his head, and his first instinct was to follow them, but another notion came to him. He rushed to the table before the waiter got there to collect the cigar butt and the man's drinking glass. He returned to his chair and calculated the time difference in New York. He dialed Agent Mendez's number as his thoughts escalated.

If my thinking is correct, this discovery could be a real game changer.

"Hey, Ramos, how's your vacation going?" Mendez asked.

"I think today may be my best day," he said excitedly and then explained his findings and gave instructions to his trusty partner.

"We need to keep a lid on this. Be careful that the boss doesn't get wind of this."

"Got you. Business as usual," Mendez agreed.

Ramos hung up the telephone and immediately went to the hotel's front desk.

"Can I speak with the manager?"

"One moment, sir. I will get him for you."

"Special Agent Ramos from the FBI Art Crime team." He displayed his badge and ID to the manager. "I am investigating a federal case, and I need a copy of the hotel video cameras. Also, I need to know the credit card information for the guests who sat at a certain table on the outside patio. I can show you," he said as they walked outside.

"Yes, sir. I will get right on it."

"Can you put a rush on it? I need it as soon as possible."

Ramos did not see the couple again during his stay, but he was hopeful that the items that were sent to the lab would line up with his hunch.

CHAPTER

36

Trouble in the Camp

Kiko barely recognized her boss, Pablo, who was sitting outside Café Italy. Unlike his usual polished, tailored look, he wore a baseball cap, a white designer jogging suit, and athletic shoes. He was unshaven, and his hair was down to his shoulders.

"Hey, I almost passed you up for a tourist." She smiled as he stood up to greet her with a kiss.

"You like my new look?"

"It is a sexy look for you," she teased.

"I am keeping a lower profile these days. How have you been?" he asked.

"Good. I had a few modeling sessions on my schedule that kept me busy."

"I have been busy, too. I am getting ready for the big race in a few weeks."

"What race?"

"The Kentucky Derby. My thoroughbred War Hammer stands a good chance to place. Would you like to come with me?"

"Gambling is your thing, not mine, but I will think about it."

"It has its ups and downs. That's why I engage in outside activities to support my expensive habits." He smiled. "It is entertaining and exhilarating. You think about it and let me know."

"I will."

"Now, tell me, how's business going? Is it running smoothly?"

"It could be better."

"What is the problem?"

"Salvador. There are growing whispers that he is a liability."

"Whispers? There are whispers about you, too. You should be able to work that out between yourselves. I thought you two had a little something going on, or were you just trying to make me jealous?"

"I like him for business purposes, but I'm not in love with him."

"Ah, a true businesswoman. You've been toying with him." He smirked.

"He has a devil-may-care attitude."

"What are you saying?"

"He's nonchalant and inattentive, which is leading to his carelessness."

"There are blurred lines that I don't understand. Are you saying you want him out of the picture?"

"Yes."

He looked for truth in her eyes, not knowing her jealousy of Grace was driving her. "Tell me what's really in your heart."

"He's a womanizer!" she shouted. "On top of that, I bet you didn't know he's stealing money from you."

"Stealing from me?"

"Exactly!" She lied with the slyness of a cat.

"Oh really? Why are you just now telling me this?"

"Because I care for you. I've been waiting for the right time to tell you." She scooted her chair closer to him."

"Do not overdo it," he cautioned.

"You knew I cared about you the first time I saw you." She batted her long false eyelashes.

"You acted like a high school girl with a crush." He smiled. "And you are an amorous lover. But I want to hear about Salvador right now," he said, with edginess in his tone.

"We don't need him. His lackadaisical attitude is going to catch up with us."

"What do you mean, 'We don't need him'? He is the best artist there is. We do need him!"

"If you want to know the truth, his apprentice, Juan, is twice as good. He is young and talented, and you would not have to pay him as much."

"I still don't get it. What is in it for you?"

Kiko's head dropped.

"Look at me!" He grabbed her chin. "You have told me lies from the moment I met you. Shall we play this game or speak the truth?"

"He's a whore!"

"Aha! Jealousy finally rears its ugly head," he laughed. "Those are strong words for someone who spreads herself too thin among older men."

"Men can be whores, too!"

"I am not denying that one bit, but don't let your feelings interfere with my business. There is no room for emotions in this operation," he reminded her. "You seem set on getting him out of the picture."

"I am working on a method where he won't feel any pain," she said with an enigmatic smile.

"You are cruel!"

"We are made from the same cloth. I am just looking out for you. It is just business," Kiko said.

His eyes got tight, and his countenance changed. "Salvador has been with me for ten years. In fact, I knew him before I met you. He may like beautiful women, but he is dependable and the best counterfeit artist the world doesn't know."

"I don't need him anymore," she spat out.

"Don't cross me!" He slapped her across the face. "And don't mess with my assets. If anything happens to him, I swear they will find pieces of your pretty little body in different parts of the world," he said angrily.

Stunned by his reaction, Kiko stood up and left like a wounded dog with its tail between its legs. She held her burning cheek and muttered, "Yes I have been your lover, your partner in crime, but you don't know my real motivation for getting so close to you. Nobody is the boss of me!"

Pablo didn't understand the depth of Kiko's sinister intentions. After she left, he considered her cold-blooded attitude and her restlessness, which convinced him to watch his own back.

CHAPTER

37

Kiko's Plan

Despite Pablo's warning, Kiko carried out her demonic plan. She whispered to her friend, sitting at the bar of Luigi's Restaurant near Milan, Italy.

"OK," the friend responded, "now that you have paid for it, when do you want this to happen?"

"Any time after now!" she said and then walked toward Olu, Salvador, and Juan, who were sitting at a nearby table.

"Nice job so far, everybody," Kiko announced. "However, the boss suggested that we should lie low on the operation."

"I agree we should slow down. When the Feds picked me up, they sounded like they were on to us," Olu said.

"It was just getting good," Salvador said to Juan, who was a little toasted after three drinks.

While Salvador and Juan were talking, Kiko deviously sprinkled a powdered mixture into Salvador's glass.

"Let's drink to our future success." Kiko raised her glass.

Juan mistakenly picked up Salvador's glass, which was close to him on his right side. Kiko noticed and inwardly panicked.

"A toast to the best artist team in the world." Olu clinked glasses with the others.

"Juan, you are one fine craftsman. What would I do without you?" Salvador said.

"Man, I am just trying to follow in your footsteps." Juan wiped the slobber suddenly dripping from his mouth. "One day, I hope to paint as well as you. Excuse me—I have to go to the john." Juan rose too quickly from the table by pushing upward with one hand, causing his other hand to slip, and he fell to the floor.

"Are you all right?" Salvador held him up. Juan's body weight pulled them both to the floor.

Kiko shouted for help. The friend at the bar had prearranged this moment. Within ten minutes, an ambulance arrived. The paramedics took Juan's vitals, placed him on a stretcher, and drove him to the hospital. Kiko put on her best distressed face, but inside, she panicked that her plan had backfired.

Salvador knew, when Kiko would not look him in the eyes, that her behavior pointed in the direction of foul play.

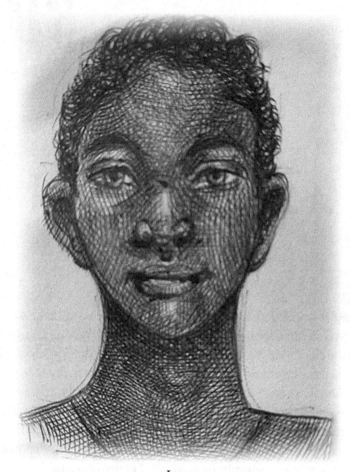

Juan

CHAPTER
38

A Floating Problem

Fear rose in Kiko's heart as she listened to the morning news.

"A fisherman spotted a body in the Po River and reported it around seven o'clock last night," the newscaster said. "Emergency teams searched the river and found a body, identified as twenty-five-year-old Juan Vasquez from Guayama, Puerto Rico. The carabinieri are investigating this incident as a homicide, based on the toxic chemicals found in his body. There are no suspects at this time. We will have a complete story for you at ten o'clock tonight. Reporting live for Radiotelevisione Italiana, this is Lorenzo Romano."

Kiko dialed Pablo's number. "We have a problem."
"What kind of a problem?" Pablo asked.

"I am watching the news. They found Juan's body in the Po River yesterday."

"What the hell happened?"

"I don't know. They said more news at ten. We had dinner the other night, and that was the last time I saw him."

"Who had dinner?"

"Me, Salvador, Olu, and Juan got together. Juan started feeling sick, and we called an ambulance. They took him to the hospital."

"Lie to yourself but tell me the truth! What did you do, Kiko?"

She reluctantly told him the entire story.

"Didn't I tell you not to mess with my assets?"

"I didn't. Salvador is still alive," she said innocently.

"But you tried to take him out!" Pablo yelled. "That was a poorly thought-out idea. Does Salvador suspect the drink was intended for him?"

"I don't know. I called him, but he didn't answer."

"Whore! Find him!"

"I am sorry. I just wanted—"

"You wanted things your way. Now look at the attention you are bringing to us. Do you recall that my last order to you was to lie low?" he shouted, infuriated with her.

"I am concerned about Salvador," said Kiko.

"It is a little late for that," he snapped. "It is said that what you did yesterday stays with you today."

"The police will be looking for me too," she surmised. "What should I do?"

"You got yourself into this hot mess. Figure it out!" Pablo slammed the telephone down.

～

Meanwhile on a narrow street in Italy, the FBI, wearing windbreakers, and with a search warrant in hand, pulled up at Salvador's main studio. After several knocks and no answer, they broke the door down. Salvador was nowhere to be found. The police seized stolen art and other items critical to the investigation. Among the items were photos of Grace. Special Agent Lillian Sanders called Ramos to report the latest findings.

CHAPTER 39

Jezebel Nightmare

In Salvador's dream, he heard Kiko's voice calling out, "Elijah! Elijah!" She screamed the words as she chased him down the road. Just as she was about to slay him, he slipped and fell—and Salvador woke up in a cold sweat. Although he was not a churchgoing man, he knew some scripture and the biblical story of Jezebel and Elijah.

Jezebel, King Ahab's wife, was an evil woman who despised Elijah, the prophet. In his despair Elijah ran and hid in a cave, where he cried out to God.

What a significant similarity. Could this dream be prophetic? Salvador wondered. *Was this God's way of getting my attention?*

Salvador did his own crying out to the Lord. "I know I behaved foolishly. I am at my wit's end. Lord, help me!" he cried.

Visibly shaken by the dream and the circumstances surrounding

Juan's death, Salvador searched for answers. It was evident to him that the deadly drink was meant for him. He recalled a former conversation with Kiko—she had threatened to kill him, but she laughed it off. The scary part was that she almost had succeeded. It was within her malicious nature. He knew by now that his part in the art scheme was exposed, with adverse consequences lurking. Like the prophet Elijah, he looked for a place to hide.

As a child, Salvador, a gifted artist, was trained by the master artists. As a young man, he was known in Italy for his great portraits. It was greed that turned his extraordinary talents toward duplicating expensive, historic artwork. A beautiful but obnoxious woman had sweet-talked him and swayed his moral character. At first, Salvador had no knowledge of the art-theft business, other than he was hired to paint a replica of whatever was asked of him and was handsomely paid in cash. He asked no questions and enjoyed his lavish lifestyle of parties, beautiful women, and a house on the French Riviera. Now, his future was in limbo.

He turned to some friends of his parents, Christopher and Ann Byrd, an American couple he had lived with while he attended college in Pontormo Village in Florence, Italy. He thought this as a place of refuge. The news of Juan's drowning had reached their ears before Salvador arrived. They approached him that evening for the truth.

"Is there something you need to share with us, son?"

He stumbled for the right words to say.

"You can talk to us. Let us make it easy for you. We heard about your apprentice, Juan. It is all over the news."

"But I didn't kill anyone. I am innocent," he insisted.

"Then why are you here? You could have turned yourself in to straighten everything out. That would have been the right thing to do."

"I had to run. I knew the authorities would come after me because I was one of the individuals last seen with him. Kiko tried to kill me, but it backfired and—"

"Slow down and tell us what happened—from the beginning."

Salvador recalled the events of previous days and how he got mixed up in a reprehensible undertaking with corrupt people.

"It all started a few years ago when I painted a portrait of a gorgeous model named Kiko. She befriended me and inched her way into my life and lured me into a place of complacency." Salvador explained the art scheme. "I had no idea it would get out of control like this."

"But you had to know, once you got involved, that it was illegal."

"Yes. Ten years ago, when I was a starving artist, an opportunity landed in my lap, and I jumped on it. A rich man took interest in my work; he saw my talent and brought me out of the muck and mire. He introduced me to a lavish lifestyle that became comfortable, and I did not want to give it up. I knew there was a price I would have to pay someday, but the only time I could relate to was *now*."

"What did you do for him?"

"When it comes to art, I did a little bit of everything."

"You know nothing easy comes without sacrificing something," Christopher said.

"Yes, it looks like my career is on the line." Salvador frowned. "I was doing OK until Kiko came into the picture a few years ago. She introduced me to her business partner with some lucrative creative ideas, and business took off in another direction."

"What type of creative ideas?"

"I was hired to paint replicas of the masters' artworks. They took the art I painted and sold it to their clients for hundreds of thousands of dollars. It was all fine at first. The paychecks were good; I could not refuse them. Then Kiko became possessive of my time. Nobody controls my time! She was jealous of every woman I painted, and that was a problem. I bought her everything, but that still was not enough. She was a manipulator, and she took advantage of my kindness and talents. I did not know things were so bad that she would try to poison me. Maybe she was stringing me along and paying me back for all the times I looked at other ladies.

"But her plan backfired. Juan accidentally picked up my glass at dinner a few nights ago, and he immediately fell to the floor. He was rushed to the hospital. Kiko would not look me in the eye during that tense moment, and that is when I figured out the drink was meant for me. She told me not to worry about Juan, that he would be OK. It was only after I heard the news report—that they found his body in the Po River—that I knew in my heart of hearts that Kiko had something to do with it. I panicked because I knew Kiko would spin the story her way. And then I had that dreadful dream and fear entered my heart."

"Why would she want to kill you?"

"I don't know her motive."

"You know, this is a risk for us to harbor you. The people you are in bed with are wicked and dangerous and could bring danger to us as well. Your alliance with her and others got you in this predicament."

"I have no other place to go."

"You are a smart man. We know you can discern good from evil. Integrity should be the foundation of what you do from this point. You cannot continue to be a senseless man. Your parents taught you better. Just turn yourself in. This is not a battle you have to fight yourself. This is where God steps in to help, if you let him."

"You don't know the powerful people I am dealing with. I stole from many rich and famous people. Kiko is vindictive, and I know she will not stop until I am dead. I cannot do this anymore."

"Sounds like excuses to me. I tell you this because we love you. You said you prayed to God, right?"

"Yes, but this will diminish my reputation. This shouldn't be my closing act," Salvador cried.

Agent Ramos stepped into the room. "This doesn't have to be your closing act. This is the beginning of your redemption."

Salvador stepped backward. "Is this a setup?"

"No! They had nothing to do with me being here, except that we knew you would eventually come back to where you felt safe," Agent Ramos said.

"Who is *we*?"

Agent Ramos flashed his badge. "I am with the FBI Art Crime team. We staked out the Byrds' place and had their phones tapped in case you came here."

"I trusted you." Salvador shook his head in disgust at the Byrds.

"We are sorry, son. We had no idea about this operation until Agent Ramos arrived just moments before you."

"You could have warned me."

"You know, stretching the truth won't make it last any longer. Give yourself up," Christopher suggested. "You cannot run forever."

"I heard what you told the Byrds, and I believe that you got caught up in the art scheme," Agent Ramos said. "Now, it's time to tell the truth. And by the way, you are right about Kiko. She is covering her own ass and has placed all blame on you. So where does that leave you but to tell the truth?"

Salvador stared into space, contemplating his next move.

"The whys and wherefores don't matter anymore. Proverbs 12:15 says, 'A wise man is he who listens to counsel.' The Byrds' love you. This is a pulsating battle between good and evil, and it is time you choose," Agent Ramos advised.

"I don't have a choice, do I?"

"Some people are never rehabilitated, but you don't seem the criminal type. We knew you were the most popular and best portrait painter in Italy and hoped you could lead us to artists in the region to find out who was painting the replicas. That's why we set up the scene at the Blikje Button Cafe with Grace."

"Grace is part of this? "Salvador gazed in astonishment at Agent Ramos.

"Yes. She has a rare passion for catching those behind the art theft operation. It did not just begin with you. She has been on this path a long time," Ramos replied.

"I was shaken when I heard about the LAI tool Grace designed, but my team said they had it under control. They told me not to worry because it would not foil our operation. They had an antidote for it."

"And you trusted their word?" Ramos said with raised eyebrows.

"I did."

"You are a fool! This has been an aggressive mission. Did you really think you wouldn't get caught?"

"I admit that a guilty feeling rose in my conscience while I was painting Grace. I sensed a modest and humble spirit. It was not just her beauty that captivated me; it was her innocence," Salvador said.

"Your conscience should have been enough for you to make things right. What you are involved in has blocked your future endeavors in art and will continue until you take intentional actions to change things," Christopher told him. "You know I care for you like a son."

"I hear you and know you are speaking the truth," Salvador said.

"We have recorded everything you said already. Now, it requires you to humble yourself and admit your part in this operation," Agent Ramos added.

"My life is futile because I have hurt so many people. Do you think Grace will forgive me?"

"She won't be happy to hear about all those photos of her we discovered at your house. What is that all about?"

"I have nothing further to say until I speak with my attorney."

Agent Ramos handcuffed him and walked him out to the car. "Get in." He shoved Salvador into the back seat.

"What about Olu?" Salvador asked.

"What of him?" Agent Ramos inquired.

"He was part of this operation."

"He was arrested today. What we want is the head of this operation. I need his name."

"I don't know his name. I just do the work that is given to me," said Salvador.

"You might as well come all the way clean. You will get less jail time."

"I never met him!"

"Who sets up the work for you?"

"It is delivered by FedEx to keep names and locations private."

"We will see how far this lie takes you." Agent Ramos slammed the door and walked over to the driver's seat.

Salvador recalled a Bible verse—Psalm 23:3—and prayed to God: "He restoreth my soul; He leadeth me in the path of righteousness for His name's sake …."

"What did you say?" Agent Ramos asked.

"I was saying a prayer."

"Yeah, you are going to need as many prayers as you can remember."

SEASON 7

The Truth Sets You Free

CHAPTER 40

The Bare Truth

The DNA report disclosed timetables and detailed facts that left Agent Ramos scratching his head. The fingerprints on file taken from the warehouse stakeout with Grace and Ellona, years ago, had the same DNA as that retrieved from the cigar butt and the glass that Ramos picked up at the Grand Hotel Tremezzo. The tapes from the hotel camera and credit card information were the final clues that cinched it. The man he was chasing, allegedly dead, was Azul, using his newly acquired name, Pablo Luza.

Agent Ramos remembered that the coroner's report was vague back then, naming Azul as one of the two victims who had been burned to a crisp in the car crash at the Wellington Holmes Art Academy many years ago. Agent Ramos wondered how the information was fabricated—and how had he dodged death? This put a whole new spin on the word *cliffhanger*. In the words of a famous TV personality and legal analyst, this news was a bombshell!

Agent Ramos reported his discovery to his boss, Amare Jackson, and eagerly reopened Azul's art-theft case. The mystifying element with no answer, was Kiko's connection to Azul. He dreaded telling Wellington and Grace the news, but that was the ugly part of his job. He hesitantly dialed Grace's cell phone.

"Grace, it's Agent Ramos."

"Hey. I was going to call you. I just heard about Salvador's apprentice, Juan. He was found in the Po River."

"Yes, I know. Our team is on top of the case and are questioning Salvador."

"What? Not Salvador. I bet that Kiko had something to do with it."

"It is under investigation. But we have a more serious issue to deal with right now. Is Wellington home?"

"Yes."

"I need to talk with you two. Tell him I will be there in ten minutes. This cannot wait." He hung up the telephone.

Ten minutes later, Grace opened the door, and Agent Ramos strode in quickly, removing his famously worn black hat.

"You didn't waste any time getting here," Wellington said. "This must be important."

Agent Ramos bit his tongue before he began explaining. "You remember I tried to catch Azul in art embezzlement deals. Then he died."

Grace sighed. "How well we know."

"Folks, I have alarming news to tell you—Azul is alive."

"What? Are you serious? I saw him die in the crash, and they confirmed that in the autopsy report!" Grace exclaimed.

"They confirmed there were two bodies in the car. The problem is nobody took the time to identify the bodies. They assumed it was Azul and Stoney. Somebody did not follow through. Bad police work, and I feel responsible."

"Damn! How did you find out?" Wellington asked.

"I was given a tip by an informant who is in prison serving hard time. He had information he was willing to give in exchange for a shorter sentence. I thought he provided information on another criminal I was looking for. I went on a vacation to Italy and was going to Monte Carlo to find this man. I was chilling on the pool patio and saw a person who got my attention. I thought I was tripping. My speculation grew when some familiarity about him set in. I had to follow my intuition. I collected some DNA and sent it to the laboratory. After research, I also found out that the bodies in the car were Stoney and an unidentified man. With some detective work and DNA, I was able to put it all together. You cannot imagine my surprise when I found out that the man in Italy was actually Azul. I didn't recognize him at first because he'd had facial reconstruction surgery and had set up a new identity. How he survived the crash is a miracle."

"This is absurd!" Grace cried.

"My sentiments exactly! I have no idea how he pulled this off. He's a diabolical criminal who just won't die."

"I have a painful memory of him from the day he was chasing me." Grace sighed as she closed her tear-filled eyes. "I almost died."

"Not to mention that he tried to kill me." Wellington made an angry face. "Wait till I get my hands on him. I am going to make him pay," he said.

"Wellington, slow down," Ramos said. "You do not want to think like that. It might cause you unwanted anxiety. This needs to be planned wisely. We cannot arrest him just yet. There is more to uncover. Leave this work to the professionals. We will handle it. Azul's new name is Pablo Luza. Here's a picture of him." Agent Ramos produced a photo from his coat pocket. "He was vaguely recognizable even after all the plastic surgery. He always had a highly active imagination, and now he's putting it to use by running new schemes."

"That is probably why he hasn't bothered us. I would not be surprised if he's been watching us since Grace's new tool hit the market," Wellington surmised.

Grace frowned. "Now there's a scary thought."

"He's also acquired many enemies. He has a villa in Monte Carlo and other residences that make him elusive. I always felt the art embezzlement operation had the feel of Azul, but I could not tie it to him because we assumed he was dead. This makes me question whether Ty Hamilton may have his hands in this operation and has kept Azul afloat all these years."

"Is there a connection?"

"Not that we know of—yet. We have irrefutable evidence that this Pablo has been linked to art theft for the last ten years. Somehow, he outfoxed us."

"I want retribution. You know we are judged by the strength of our enemies," Wellington added.

"That saying may be true, but God is our strength, and this battle is not ours; it belongs to Him. And we will come out on top," Grace concluded.

"You've said a mouthful, honey. I feel responsible. But I don't want you to worry."

"I hope Ty is not involved." Grace sat forward on the sofa and ran her fingers nervously through her hair.

"I spoke with Monica about Ty, but haven't told her about Azul. I have surveillance in and around her house. It will reveal anything we may need to know about Ty, and will protect her from Pablo," Ramos said. "Azul has always been slippery, but we will catch this fool and put him away once and for all. Expect a call from me soon." Agent Ramos got up to leave. "I will contact Monica and let her know everything that I shared with you."

After he left, a heaviness hung in the room. It was like a two-hundred-pound weight had come to visit their lives.

"Grace, you know we will get through this," Wellington assured her.

A blank expression remained on Grace's face.

"A man once said, 'A woman who has much to say and says nothing can be deafening.'"

"I heard you." Grace slumped into the sofa. "I am at a loss for words."

CHAPTER 41

Radiance's Questions

Radiance stood quietly on the stairs, listening to Agent Ramos's conversation with her parents. A while later, she came downstairs and walked into Grace's home studio. She watched as Grace stood motionless before a blank canvas.

"Are you OK, Mommy?" Radiance asked.

"Yes, I am fine. Why do you ask?" Grace appeared calm.

"Mom, I have been standing here for a couple of minutes, watching you in a daze."

"I'm fine, dear. I'm thinking about something."

"I overheard the conversation." Radiance took a nearby seat.

That got Grace's attention. She grabbed Radiance's hand. "What did you hear?" Grace asked, her eyes displaying concern.

"I heard him say something about art theft and some criminals and then—I didn't want to hear anything else, so I slipped back upstairs."

"Sweetie, it's Agent Ramos's job to report things that concern us. We have talked about this."

"Talked about what?"

"The illegal dealings that go on in the art world. This is not new to you. I know you studied that in your art history class. Didn't you?"

"Yes, we have an assignment due right now in Art History about art and criminology."

"Perfect. This is a good time to do some research and check out the evolution of criminology in the art world."

"My concern is the tone of your voice when you were talking to Agent Ramos. I never heard you sound so terrified."

"I know. Hearing that news for the first time was shocking to me, and I admit it is frightening, too. I understand your concern, but Agent Ramos and his team are trained for these missions."

"But Mom, you have been in a situation like this before. Why is this happening all over again?"

"Darling, I have a passion to fight for justice for artists. You understand that, don't you? God gives me the grace to go through this."

"Yes, but you are the only mom I have, and I don't want anything to happen to you." Radiance's eyes filled with tears. "I'm afraid."

Grace pulled her close and held her tight. A moment passed between them before Grace spoke. "I want to assure you that your dad and I are not going to be in harm's way. We would not do anything to put you, Javier, or any of us at risk. We love you and will protect you through this situation and anything in life that we face. We cannot control what evil people do, but we can make a difference. That difference will be made through the LAI tool. That is why I created it. We will let technology do its job. And you don't need to worry. I won't play Super Woman this time around." Grace smiled.

"You promise?"

"Easier said than done, but that is my goal."

"What are you and Dad going to do?"

"Exactly what Agent Ramos recommended—do nothing until we hear back from him. We trust him, and our confidence is in God, who will fight this battle for us."

"God must really love you."

"Yes, he loves us, and he's got this," Grace assured her. "Now, young lady, I don't want you to worry or to fear." Grace kissed her on the cheek. "I think you have art history homework, don't you?" She walked Radiance toward the door.

"Yes, and I'm going to be paying closer attention to what Dad says—I mean Professor Holmes—since my family is making history." She grinned.

"I trust you and Javier to keep our family information confidential," Grace smiled as she gently touched her shoulder.

CHAPTER 42

Angel Alert

Grace thought about her conversation with Radiance and realized that there were two other angels in her life with whom she needed to talk about the current circumstance—her mother and her best friend, Ellona.

She parked her Mercedes and entered Spa 52.

Ellona greeted her at the door. "Grace. I'm surprised to see you. You always call first."

"I'm not here for a spa treatment or to shoot the breeze. We need to talk." Grace pushed past her to sit down.

"You sound serious." Ellona took a seat at the front desk.

"I am. You will never guess who resurfaced," Grace said, not wasting words.

After a long pause, Ellona said, "OK, I give up. Who?"

"The devil himself—Azul."

"What?" Ellona covered her mouth to hold in the scream and held a crazy-eyed gaze.

"Yes, Azul. It is surreal. We both witnessed the fiery crash. How many times have we relived that day? How he escaped is beyond me. It's like he had some superpowers or something."

"You know the devil thinks he does. How do you know this?" Ellona inquired.

"Agent Ramos told us. He has been investigating art theft related activity for some time and trying to find the mastermind behind it. He got a tip, and he did some DNA work, and the results came back positive as Azul's."

"Girl, you got to be lying."

"I wish to God I was. Azul changed his identity, got facial reconstruction, and now his name is Pablo Luza." Grace showed her the picture Ramos had sent to her cell phone.

"Girl, that man is still fine. I like that salt-and-pepper thing he got going on. I could not imagine him looking any better. But damn!"

"Girl, you need to focus on what I'm saying. It's serious." Grace snatched the cell phone from her. "Agent Ramos believes he is the mastermind behind a new art theft ring. The underlying reality is that he is alive and dangerous! I'm surprised he hasn't revealed himself to us in all these years. I am sure he definitely has been watching us from a distance."

"Does this mean I need to watch my back?" Ellona asked.

"Let's hope that we are little fish in a big pond. If he wanted us, he would have gotten to us by now. He's operating on a much larger scale. Agent Ramos and his team are close to apprehending him, so we cannot do anything stupid. You hear me?"

"You saying the shit is about to hit the fan?"

"Yes, something like that. And I do not want you in the middle of it. The moment Pablo finds out that Agent Ramos knows his identity, the dance will be on."

"I have to admit that it's been a while since I had a man who loved me like he did. I would not mind lying next to that sexy, lean, athletic body just one more time."

"Have you lost your mind?" Grace shook Ellona's shoulders. "That's warped thinking. I promise you that he hasn't changed. Personally, Azul was charming, but spiritually, he is corrupt. Besides, I thought you and Max were hitting it hard."

"We are. You know men these days; they don't want to commit. So we continue playing these love games. The story of my life."

Grace rolled her eyes. "The thing that concerns me is that our friend Monica may be in the middle of this."

"What do you mean?"

"Agent Ramos strongly believes Ty may be involved."

"Oh God! That is not good. Does Monica know?"

"Not yet, but the FBI has all our houses under surveillance, including Ty's. It is alarming news, but we won't back down. Same devil then, same devil now. The difference is that this time, Pablo is running out of time."

"He is probably angry about your new tool and waiting for the right time to strike, don't you think? You know he's got a plan."

"Yeah, maybe. I believe that Kiko chick is part of the plan. If she tries anything else, she is going to get a taste of my special 'Grace sauce.'"

"Sista girl, hold up!" Ellona bent over with laughter. "What do you need me to do?"

"Nothing. I just wanted to let you know." Grace paused and then said, "Come to think of it, there may be one thing you can do. Radiance overheard our conversation with Agent Ramos, so I may call on you to keep her concealed from all of this."

"No problem. Although you know I like action and want to be involved, I promise to lie low this time."

"Will you?" Grace rolled her eyes again.

Ellona uncrossed her legs, opened her desk drawer, and pulled out a Smith & Wesson .357 Magnum revolver. "If you need backup, I got you, girl."

Grace shook her head in disbelief.

"What?" Ellona asked. "I need to be ready, girl. Like you said, it's personal!"

~

Grace dialed her mother's number. It rang a few times before Ruth picked up.

"Hey, Mom, how are you? I always call when I need to hear your sweet voice."

"I am always happy to hear your voice too, baby."

"I need your ear again."

"I am all ears."

"Mom, I am tired and running out of energy in this fight."

"Sweetheart, what is happening now? Is it that tool that's giving you a headache or a heartache?"

"It is much bigger than that. The good news is that the tool has gone from making inroads to making great strides in the art community."

"Congratulations. Your father and I knew you would do something significant, something that would make a difference in others' lives. What has you discouraged?"

"A huge development and a threat to our lives."

"It cannot be anything that God didn't already know. So while it looks big to us—"

"Mom, stop! I don't mean to be disrespectful or cut you off. I know you always look at the brighter side of things and see them spiritually, but this problem is physical right now."

"What is it, dear?"

"Azul is alive! He escaped the crash."

"Oh my! Sounds like déjà vu. First, Wellington was pronounced dead, but he lived. Now you are telling me Azul has come back from the dead?"

"It is true. He escaped the crash and has been in hiding for many years. Can you believe it?" Grace cried.

"I can see why you are upset. Is it the threat of the tool that made him reappear?"

"I am sure that is a threat to his thriving business. Agent Ramos discovered him." Grace relayed the entire story to her mother. "Azul was not counting on anyone finding out his new identity. My strength to move forward is stifled," Grace whined.

"As a Christian, you will face opposition and even persecution. No weapon formed against you and Wellington will prosper. You are on assignment, according to the will of God. You walk in authority, without any apology, because the power and authority has been given you, according to the word of God. He will protect you against evil manifestations. But don't fear!" Ruth reminded her. "You know I always have a good word for you, don't you?"

"Yes, that's why I called."

"Aunt Sis always says, 'He ain't the only pebble on the beach.'" Ruth laughed. "There is value in your trials. Know God will not give you more than you can bear. He knows you will make it through, and He will take care of Azul. Here is another word from Isaiah 40:31. It says, 'Those who hope in the Lord will renew their strength. They will soar on wings like eagles. They will run and not grow weary; they will walk and not be faint.'"

"Are you still hoping in the Lord?"

"More than ever. Whom do I have besides Him? He is my strength and my song. Although this is a difficult season, keep focused on your divine purpose. God is faithful to what He called you to do."

"Once again, thanks, Mom. You are an angel. I always cherish your wisdom and encouragement."

"I love you, and I am here for you." Ruth blew her a kiss through the telephone.

CHAPTER 43

Monica's Response

Agent Ramos dialed Monica's number, praying for the right words to explain the startling development.

"Hey, Monica. You got a moment? I need to share something with you."

"I hope it's not more about Ty. I don't know how much more I can handle."

"No. It's about our old friend Azul. There is no way to tell you this other than—he is alive. He didn't die in the crash."

Monica gasped. "No way! Do Grace and Wellington know?"

"Yes. I told them already. There is more. I believe that Azul may have involved Ty in his new businesses since he has resurfaced under a new name and identity."

"I feel deceived. First Ty, and now Azul. That's way too much information."

"We are not jumping to conclusions until we find out all the facts. Azul's new name is Pablo Luza. He got facial reconstruction and doesn't look the same. I will text his photo."

"I may have seen him and didn't even know it. Is my life in danger?"

"I am not sure, but I am here to help you uncover the truth."

Monica sighed heavily. "I really hope Ty is not involved in this."

"Me too, but I know when someone is part of an organization like that, it is considered family, and it is hard to break away from them. Ty got out of the relationship once before, but Pablo may have pulled him back in," said Ramos.

"I noticed some strange behavior from Ty lately. He has been very secretive about his telephone calls. On one occasion, when we were out having dinner, I saw him talking to a gentleman, but he did not introduce me. At the time, I did not think anything of it. For all I know, that could have been Pablo."

"I would presume that by now, with all the questions you've asked him, he suspects you know something," Agent Ramos said.

"I have a feeling he does. I haven't seen him for a few days, but I'm seeing him this evening."

"I have conclusive information that points to Pablo's organization, and I want you to be careful. Both of them could be facing grand theft charges if found guilty."

"Oh God, what have I gotten myself into?"

"Nothing that won't be resolved, and I hope that will be very soon. You have the natural instinct of a detective. You used it before, and I trust that you will do so again."

"Yes, but this time, it's different. It is my personal life, and my emotions are involved. It might be time for me to purchase a gun."

"I am not telling you to do that, but I won't tell you *not* to. I know he loves you, and I believe he won't harm you."

"It's not him I'm worried about. Azul has been alive these

years," she said sadly, with fear rising in her heart. "I pray that Ty is not involved."

"Remember," Agent Ramos said, "I have eyes and ears everywhere."

CHAPTER

44

Talk Is Cheap

The romantic candlelight setting was ill-timed for the conversation Monica planned.

Ty was singing George Benson's "Love Ballad"—"What we have is much more than they can see"—when he opened his door. "Hey, sweetie. You smell good." He took a whiff of Monica's neck, swung her around in a dance move, and then pulled her in closely.

"Am I missing an anniversary or something?" she asked.

"I thought I would prepare a nice meal and set the mood for a lovely evening with the woman I love." He embraced her tighter.

"That's thoughtful of you," she said, releasing his hold and sitting down at the table. "How was your day?" she asked.

"Uneventful, besides setting this up for you. How was yours?" Ty poured a glass of Chardonnay for Monica and himself.

"Probably more eventful than yours. I had lunch with a friend and heard some news that sounded suspect. I'm unsure how much of it is true," Monica said.

"What kind of news?" he asked, taking a sip of wine.

"When I first met you, I said that the most important elements for entering a relationship were transparency and trust. Remember that?" She searched his eyes.

"Yes, I remember talking about it."

"I am praying that transparency and trust is still our bond."

"Yes of course it is. Where is this conversation going?" He swallowed hard.

"Somewhere along the way, maybe you failed to tell me something important about yourself."

"I believe I've told you everything."

"But you left out an important piece."

"What piece is that?"

"Your rich, powerful, and ruthless business associates."

"Why do you want to talk about all of my acquaintances? I know a lot of people all over the world."

"Need I mention some shady and illegal dealings y'all are involved in? Let us say, for example, stolen or traded art. Does any of that ring a bell?"

"Monica, baby, you must have gotten some misinformation from someone."

"I don't think so. I feel that everything you have said to me has been a lie. Is there a dark side of you that you are not sharing with me?"

"OK. OK. Let's talk. Why are you trying to ruin this beautiful dinner I planned for you?"

"I believe it is a little late for talking. You have been pulling on my heartstrings long enough. And now I have no more time or heart to give you."

"What are you talking about, woman? We just sat down for a nice dinner, and for some odd reason, you have a lot of accusations. Why?"

"I've realized I may not know you as well as I thought I did."

"Monica!" He rose from his seat. "What has gotten into you, and who are you listening to?"

"I want to hear the truth—that's who I want to listen to." She raised her voice. "The truth! I suspect that you are caught up in an underhanded operation, and that, my dear, has direct impact on my life career, my future, and now, my emotional stability. Somehow, over time, you knowingly dragged me into this. I could possibly get hurt." She frowned, trying to contain her emotions.

"Monica, the last thing I want to do is hurt you. You have to believe me."

"Is it important that I do?"

"Yes. That day you walked into the Johansson Gallery, when I first laid eyes on you, all I could see was a beautiful lady I was attracted to. I also thought you might be someone who could rescue me from myself. Is that so wrong? Everyone has a good and a not-so-good side. I wanted you to see the good side of me—and you did." He moved closer to her than she liked.

Monica was disturbed. "Tell me who you are, and exactly what you do, and who you work with. And are you saying you are involved in rogue operations?"

"Listen. I sense your level of anxiety, but it is more complicated than you know."

"Was this about protecting yourself, and that's why you kept it from me?"

"No, that's not true." He tried to calm her.

"Why didn't you trust me enough to talk to me? I opened my heart to you and told you my entire life. This breaks my heart." She held back the tears forming in her eyes.

"Baby, why are you crying? I haven't done anything wrong. I know I am not making much sense, but it's not what you think. This takes time to explain."

"When is the right time?"

"Not now!"

"I see you are someone I don't know at all," she said, outraged at his coolness. "Explain to me why you continue to drag our relationship on?"

"Because I love you," he said, reaching for her hand.

She snatched it back. "No matter what your heart said, your actions say something different. It is like I am seeing you for the first time. What happened to you?"

"Monica, you know I love you, and I am working on straightening out everything else in my life so that we will be happy for the rest of our lives," he insisted.

"You knew I was vulnerable. You quietly slipped into the tender depths of my heart. How could you do this to me?" she cried.

"I don't know what to say to make this right. I didn't plan on falling in love with you, but I don't regret it. These have been the best years of my life."

"I cannot trust you. There is nothing you can say that I will believe."

"Who are you getting information from anyway?" he snapped.

"Does it matter, if it's true?"

"You need to hear the whole story."

"I've heard nothing from you yet to convince me that you are not guilty of something. I took a big risk in opening my heart up to you, and now you have crushed it."

"Monica, please!"

She pushed away from him.

"Don't go!" He grabbed her by the hand. "I could not tell you everything because I didn't want to lose you."

"There you go again—it's all about you. It sounds so familiar. I have been clinging to hope, but it is pointless." She pulled away and walked out the door.

Ty was left hearing the screeching tires of her Mercedes. He knew in his heart that he was losing her. What he didn't know was how to fix things and make them right again.

Ty had no ideas that Agent Ramos had caught the conversation on tape. It was a starting point, but was it enough?

CHAPTER 45

Fragmented Heart

"Nothing can undo the embarrassment or pain I feel," Monica explained to Grace. "In my anger, I did not even recognize my own voice because it was at such a high pitch when I was talking to him." She wiped her red, swollen eyes.

"It's a shame one can look so good on the outside, but the inside is all jacked up," Grace said.

"The frustrating truth is, the moment I looked him in the eye, I knew he was lying and that he had hidden a lot of this from me."

"Monica, don't do this! I am the one who urged you to date him. You may be judging him too early. Maybe the next time you speak to him, give him a chance to explain. We need as much information as we can get. Maybe he can redeem himself."

"See, there you go again. Always trying to make things right and help somebody." Monica sniffed.

"I am just saying you cannot let bitterness and hate enter into your heart," Grace said. "Everything will boil to the top like sweet cream, and the truth will come out. Give it time."

"I hate that he is not telling me everything. Only then can I determine the truth for myself."

"God will reveal it. Besides, Agent Ramos is on it. I sure hope he is wrong about Ty's connection. I still want to believe he's a good brother who just got caught up. Money and power can drive you to lose control."

"Good brother, my ass. That brother may be going to jail with Azul." Monica placed her hands on her hips.

"Girl, I have never seen you so mad, let alone cuss. I am gonna get out of your way," Grace teased.

"He hasn't called me in a few days."

"His staying away points to his guilt—or that he cannot face you."

"He needs to keep his distance if he's wrong, and if I am right about it, he will." Monica said. "A huge part of our relationship is definitely broken."

"You told me a while back that the relationship became intoxicating to you. That was your first sign to take a step back. He romanced you, wooed and dined you, and the last time we talked, you were happy with him."

"Yes, and I fell into his trap. So cunning—just like the devil." Monica sighed.

"You fell in love; that's what you did. God knew what was going on and uncovered it so you would not fall through the cracks. For that, you should be thankful."

"Oh, believe me, I am singing His praises every day that that fool is on his way out of my life."

"We all fall into a trap or two. That's life. The good thing is, there's a way of escape."

"Amen to that, sista." They fist bumped. "It is strange that he didn't trust me enough to tell me the truth."

"Secrets hurt, and they cause disappointment. God heals the brokenhearted and is near to you at this difficult time. I am here for you too. Let's go to God in prayer and ask his help." Grace grabbed her hand. "Dear Lord, we know you are our Father, and friend, and you are the comforter and healer. I ask that you give my sister peace and uncover the truth as we cast this care on You. Help her through the hurt, the worry, and the pain. Help her to forgive Ty. In Jesus's name, amen." She turned to Monica. "Let's leave it at the altar and go get some ice cream. Would that make you feel better?"

"Yes. I am going to pile it on—a double-fudge sundae, maybe two scoops of chocolate, with the whipped cream and cherries on top." Monica laughed.

"Chocolate always seems to soothe the heart, doesn't it?"

Monica agreed and then said, "Do you remember when I thanked you for introducing me to Ty?"

"Yes."

"Well, I take it all back."

They laughed.

CHAPTER

46

A Plan That Seems Right

Agent Ramos admitted his ability to create major change in protecting the huge art world from crime was dismal, with only a handful of art crime officers in the US and other countries. The global art trade, being the largest unregulated business between private citizens, collectors, and proprietary interests on the planet, left no paper trail for detectives like him. It made his hard work seem hopeless and depressing at times. However, he was determined not to give up. Ramos rehearsed his defense before entering Amare Jackson's office.

"How was your vacation?" Jackson asked.

"It paid off. Are you ready for this?"

"Shoot."

"There is irrefutable evidence that Azul, now going under the assumed name Pablo Luza, is the czar behind the art theft operations."

"Azul? Wait. Wait. Wait! I thought he died years ago!?"

"We all did."

"How did you come to the conclusion that he is alive?"

"I told you I had a hunch that I needed to follow up on. It turned out to be the truth. While I was relaxing in Italy on vacation, a stroke of luck crossed my path. I saw a guy that fit the profile of the informant's report."

"Relaxing? Come on, man! Get to the point."

"Yes, relaxing. I was minding my own business, sitting on the patio, enjoying the sun, when I heard this voice. I turned and saw a man, and something about him was familiar, but I could not put my hands on it."

"What did you do?"

"He was smoking a cigar that had an awful, distinct smell. There is only one guy I know who smokes that expensive brand. My mind started reeling. When he got up from the table to leave, he left the cigar butt in the ashtray and limped away. That was my next clue. I decided to trust my razor-sharp intuition. I knew I had to retrieve that evidence. I hurried over to his table, picked the cigar butt out of the ashtray, and picked up his drinking glass before the waiter returned to the table. I also went to the manager of the hotel and asked for video footage on all their cameras. Then I called Agent Mendez with instructions, and he sent it to a lab for testing."

"You mean you and Mendez have been withholding critical information from me?"

"I had to be sure before I told you. Let me tell you the whole story before you condemn me."

"Go head, but this better be good."

"The test came back with Azul's DNA all over it. Bam!"

"Sounds like that vacation paid off," Jackson grinned.

"We are just beginning. I didn't recognize him because he got a facial reconstruction. Here is his picture." He handed it to Jackson. "This is a breakthrough moment that offers us an opportunity to try something outside of the box."

"What's that, Ramos?"

"I heard that Pablo/Azul is a manipulator and runs his business affairs with an iron fist, but this time, his habits are going to trap him," Ramos explained.

"What habits?"

"Gambling, horse racing, and pretty women. In fact, the informant told me about some stolen horses this guy is going to use in some top races. I've already made moves to track entries in events like the Kentucky Derby and other prequalifying races coming up."

"That's a familiar clue. Good analysis, Ramos. So far, you haven't messed up anything. Now, let's stick with my way of doing things. I designed this sting operation, and we need to stay with my plan," Jackson said, detailing the next steps in the operation.

They held a mutual gaze.

"You know, when someone like him loses power, there is nothing more important than getting it back. Azul re-established himself and he wants to continue his power grab," Ramos said.

"I don't disagree with that," Jackson conceded.

"My team is working their asses off, and you don't give us any credit. I am doing my best to keep them motivated, but sometimes, it all seems futile."

"Why? Because I won't do it your way? Remember, you chose this line of work. I know it is difficult because we are a limited team. Nobody said we would eliminate the world of all the criminals, and no one pays law enforcement for ridding the world of criminals. Our budgets rarely change. We need to stick with the basics."

"And what are the basics?"

"You know the drill, Ramos."

"Yeah, yeah. Nothing has worked or eliminated these fools in the past. That's why I want to try something different."

"Like I said, stick to the plan," Jackson pounded his hand on the desk.

"I've been at this for years, and sometimes, I wonder why I keep doing this," Ramos said, raising his voice.

"Who's telling you to quit?"

"I'm not quitting! I'm just saying."

"You do it because you care, and you are fed up with criminals getting away with this shit."

"Right. Somebody has to care."

"By the way, I heard about your latest inquiry with Internal Affairs. You can't seem to stay out of trouble. There is always something going on. I heard somebody shot a cop, and you beat the guy up. What is that about?" Jackson asked.

"Yes, it was a cop, a friend of mine."

"Who was he?"

"A police dog named Shorty."

"A police dog? That's what I'm talking about. You cannot always invoke violence to resolve disputes. Defending dogs is a good human-interest headline, but your reckless conduct is gonna get you killed."

"Boss, I'm just sending a message—that's all. I take responsibility for my insensitive behavior. Besides, nothing is going to distract me from my mission. Beneath the anger, I am really a peaceful guy. I used to bust heads, but now I am putting my energy into busting art thieves." He produced a half smile. "You got to admit there's an 'art' to what I do. No pun intended."

"Right. Explain that to my boss, who has your name on a lot of his 'busted' lists. Remember the next time you get ready to do something stupid that it reflects directly on me. Now get out of here, and get that crazy smile off your face!"

Ramos walked away, half listening to his boss's words and wanting to completely follow his plan. But his mind would not let him rest, and his original plan seemed right to him, even if it meant getting fired.

Ramos entered Agent Mendez's office and shook his hand, thanking him for the help with the DNA discovery of Azul. "I have a plan," he said. "This is turning into a cat-and-mouse chase, and I am tired of it. Pablo is a gambler who loves pretty women and horse racing. One of them is going to be the death of him, and I hope it is this one," Ramos smiled as he shared his strategic scheme.

SEASON 8
In Due Season

CHAPTER 47

Identity Crisis

Pablo, sitting alone at the Harlem Cigar Room, froze when he saw two big burly men sitting at the bar, trying to appear inconspicuous as they observed him. There were also two individuals prowling the place who looked like undercover agents. Nobody knew Pablo's original identity, except a few insiders, but it was getting harder to keep his secret. He had various enemies but didn't know if they were Russian, Greek, or the Mafia. Pablo always sat near a door in case he needed to make a quick exit. He made deliberate eye contact with his bodyguards at the door to signal the opposition. What he didn't expect was Agent Ramos coming up from behind and touching his shoulder.

"Azul! Or is it Pablo, my friend? We meet again, under the most unforeseeable circumstances."

"This must be a case of mistaken identity," he said.

"Oh yeah. I forgot you have selective memory." Ramos laughed. "I see you changed your name."

"Is there any crime in that?"

"There is always a crime where you are involved."

"Well, if it isn't Ramos the Rock! What brings you here?" Pablo produced a half grin.

"You always led me on a pathetic chase, but you knew I would catch up with you sooner or later."

"I was incapable of thinking that far," Pablo replied sarcastically. "I hear my friend Grace is making big-time strides."

"It seems women are one of your downfalls. Like your friend Kiko. Very much like you, she is a remorseless piece of work."

"I don't know who you are talking about."

"She is a calculated sociopath. That's what she is."

Pablo smiled. "How did you find me after all these years?" he asked coolly.

"The art theft activity looked a lot like your artistry, if that's what you want to call it. One thing I must admit that I admired about you is how you helped the homeless. That act of kindness puzzled me."

"Well, I slipped a bit. The new me was in an ambivalent state of mind at the time. You know—mixed emotions," Pablo explained.

"It is an intrinsic part of the human condition, but it was difficult to believe that you, of all people, could show heart to others. It slanted my view of the obnoxious man I knew. For that, I almost thought about forgiving all you've done."

"I would have done it for a dog, you mangy cop. What is it to you?"

"A name change, a new identity, but still the same old Azul. Ump ump ump! Haven't you heard the saying, 'A bad man is worse when he pretends to be a saint'?"

"Man, take it easy on a dude from the hood. Self-absorption is my prerogative. I had it rough when I was young. We were poor, and my father left my mother with six kids. She was an addict, and I ended up in an orphanage and had to fend for myself. That is where I learned my street trade. I related with the homeless. I wanted to be somebody and had dreams of being rich. Some luck, huh?" He laughed.

"So much for your sad story. I'm not buying it. I don't need to particularly prove you did all of this. I just want your ass off the streets and rotting in prison. I am curious, though. How'd you do it?" Ramos asked.

"Do what?"

"Escape death and start a new life?"

Pablo explained, "During the car chase with Grace and Ellona, my partner Stoney and I were headed toward the Wellington Holmes Art Academy. Moments before the crash, I foresaw the terrifying end, opened my car door, and plunged out into the street. I landed on the sidewalk, where four homeless men were sitting in their boxes. They quickly moved my badly bruised and broken body to a side street and stripped me of my expensive clothing and accessories, intending, I suppose, to leave me for dead. I was in a semiconscious state and pleaded with them for help, saying that some bad people were trying to kill me. One guy had mercy and talked the others into getting help. They put my wounded body in a long cardboard box and transported me by foot to a homeless shelter, where I was nursed back to health.

"Having access to money and resources, I connected with a reliable doctor friend, who arranged for my transportation to his facility, where he performed cosmetic reconstructive surgery. From there, I took on a whole new identity and a name change. Voilà! A new Azul emerged! How do you like me now?"

"Still the same old Azul. Arrogant and proud as ever of your own crafty plans."

"No one knew my new identity, except for a choice few. Unfortunately, my limp got worse. That was probably the biggest giveaway."

"No! It was that stinky signature cigar butt you left in the ashtray at the Grand Hotel Tremezzo, where I first saw you. I knew of only one man who smoked that brand. That was my first clue. Then I saw you limping, but it didn't look like you. I could not rest until I knew, so I had to keep searching until I got my answer. You really had me fooled, running different kinds of operations outside of art. I got a tip about a witty man involved in scandalous schemes. I followed the lead, and it led me to you. After I took a good look at the entire picture, it had your name written all over it. I just didn't figure you were alive. DNA is the best thing that has happened in my line of work."

"So you were stumped?" Pablo tried imagining that.

"Oh, but only for a moment."

"Man, I am a businessman, trying to take care of my family. I think I gave myself up by coming back to the neighborhood to the homeless. I could not resist helping them. They were generous enough to save my life. I detested the conditions they lived in and wanted to change their lives," Pablo explained.

"We also identified that body in the car. Smart move to put the body in the trunk of your car to make it appear as yours."

"That was not in the original plan," Pablo went on to explain. "That damn Stoney. I didn't know he had a person hiding in the back seat until we drove off, and then the guy's head popped up. I didn't have time to figure out what the hell Stoney was up to. I should have killed both of them, but it all worked out just fine."

"That was the one thing we never could figure out—why you would be sitting in the back when we knew you were driving. It didn't make sense. That explains it. You will still be charged for his murder too. You know, you can stop this nonsense at any time and quietly come with me."

"And end the fun of you chasing me? Ha! You got to be kidding. There's some art to what I do, and I am not through just yet. If you had enough information to arrest me, we wouldn't be sitting here, talking."

Ramos frowned but then added, "Speaking of art—man, I picked up some of your old artwork that you created years ago, and I see why they kicked your butt out of art school. The real issue is that you are just a frustrated artist!"

Pablo's face drooped. "That's not fair, man. What you going to do with my paintings?"

"I just might hang them. Just kidding." Ramos laughed heartily.

"Those paintings are for my children!"

"Ah, I didn't know you were a family man. With all your charm and charisma, I don't understand why you chose to be a serial fool. God knows your secrets, and it's finally caught up with you."

"You are jealous because I am making millions. You ain't making that much money and are probably broke right now." He laughed, causing Ramos to grit his teeth. "Besides, it appears you are working with a thin layer of information. You don't have enough compelling evidence of a crime."

"You have no idea what I am working with. Do I need to remind you of the last time I kicked your ass?"

"Man, that was an extreme abuse of power."

"I think that is subject to interpretation. I took my weapons off, and we fought street-style. That was fair play."

"You call that proper police performance?"

"You were there. We duked it out. Admit that I got a leg up on you that day."

"Touché, Ramos!"

Ramos asked. "Is Ty working for you?"

Pablo looked at him.

"Oh, you not gonna answer me? That's as damning as it gets. Don't make me whip you again."

A waitress walking pass with drinks was Pablo's perfect defense. Sensing an opening, Pablo stuck out his cane and tripped her, upsetting her tray, and mayhem erupted. This created a quick exit for Pablo out the side door. The two bodyguards fought off the suspicious visitors, while Ramos pursued Pablo, jumping, stumbling, and tripping over chairs that Pablo knocked in his path with his cane. A light breeze came in when Pablo opened the door. He stepped outside, and his breathing was intense, causing his heart to palpitate. He limped to the curb, where a young man was sitting on a Harley-Davidson. Pablo pointed his gun, poked him with his cane, and ordered him off the bike. Then he jumped on and sped away.

"You haven't seen the last of me, you devil!" Ramos yelled. He stood outside the door, with his black hat in one hand and his gun in the other. The two Russian agents, in regular clothing, were pissed. They were within a hair's breadth of catching Pablo before they met his burly bodyguards. This was a personal matter that Ramos decided would not fail. He came close this time and would not give up until Pablo was locked away for good.

~

Pablo rode a distance into the cool evening air. He pulled into an empty lot and got off the bike. In desperation he found a place to kneel and pray.

"Lord, I heard sometime in my early childhood that You are the helper. I am having a hell of a time discerning good from evil. Is it too late for me? I know I haven't been to church in a month of Sundays. Ok, maybe years," he admitted. "But can You please forgive me? Have mercy on me Lord!" Pablo begged.

God, in his boundless supply of grace, whispered, "*My son, I love you, just not what you do. I called you out of darkness, but you chose to exist there. You changed your outward identity but did not change your inward man. Repent and change.*"

Pablo pleaded, "Stay with me, Lord!"

Pablo aka Azul

CHAPTER 48

Frustration Manifested

Pablo and his bodyguards arrived at Ty's home. The interaction with Ty was tense.

"Man, I was not expecting to see you." Ty tried to control his shaky voice.

"I bet you weren't." Pablo threw his hat on the marble table. "Did you get my call?"

"No, I must have missed it," Ty lied.

"I had a run-in with Ramos."

"What? Ramos?"

Pablo pointed his cane in Ty's chest and demanded, "What the hell is going on?"

"I don't know what you're talking about."

"I think you know better than anybody else."

"Me? Why would I put myself in danger?"

"You know I hate surprises. I barely escaped arrest today. Besides you, only a few people know my real identity. How else could Ramos find me, unless you or your woman told him? It has been years since I had to worry about him, and now, that punk is on my trail. On top of that, other enemies are prowling who also want part of me. Man, I have been like a brother to you."

The color drained from Ty's face.

"You know silence can be an admission of guilt," Pablo said.

"I would never do that to you." Ty bowed his head and thought for a moment. "Damn, that's why Monica is so upset."

"What is this about Monica?"

"She asked a million questions about stolen art and whether I was mixed up in it."

"Well, what did you tell her?"

Ty trembled, breathing heavily. "Of course, I played it off, but that didn't stop her from blowing up. I swear I did not tell anyone about you."

"There are too many coincidences at the same time. Why did I trust you with my life again?" Pablo shouted.

"I promise you—I'm not the one."

"I can see the lie in your eyes." Pablo pushed Ty up against the wall with his cane.

Ty, fearing Pablo's anger, ran out of the house—but bumped into the chests of two huge bodyguards. They beat him to a pulp, leaving him bleeding and crawling on the concrete driveway.

Pablo limped over to him and kicked him in the face. "This is where cruelty and fear shake hands, my friend."

CHAPTER 49

Last Chance for Love

Monica looked through her peephole and reluctantly opened the door. Ty was slumped over and bleeding profusely. His bloody hands pushed against the door as she dragged his heavy body and helped him to the closest chair.

"Ty, what happened? You know you shouldn't be here."
"I have nowhere else to go. He's trying to kill me."
"Who's trying to kill you?"
"Pablo."
"What happened?"
"I will explain later. Whatever you do, don't call the police."
"I will call Agent Ramos. He will know what to do."
"No! Don't call him either."
"Did anyone follow you here?"

"I don't think so. They beat me and left me."
"Who's they?"
"Pablo and his bodyguards."

Monica went into the bathroom and got a washcloth and first-aid kit to clean his wounds. She sat sullenly on a kitchen stool while Ty explained the entire story. Monica was fearful of the revelation, but she relaxed, knowing the bugging device Ramos had placed in her home was capturing everything. It did not stop her from going through the range of emotions—rage, anger, confusion, and emotional pain. The conversation finally came to a boiling point.

"You could have cleared your name and put any unfounded suspicion to rest a long time ago, but you didn't. I get it! You could not because you were part of the problem. You deceived everybody—Grace, Wellington, and the Johanssons—and to think you acted like they were your best friends. You also knew about the painting, *The Amnesty*, and probably were involved in the art scheme with Pablo. How could you? Was giving donations to Wellington to rebuild his art academy your way of getting rid of your guilt? Shame on you!"

"I have to admit I felt redemption by giving back to a worthy cause."

"You didn't answer my question."

"Which one?"

"*The Amnesty*—were you part of Pablo's scheme at the Johansson Gallery?"

Ty was quiet.

"I see now that my perception about you is correct. You have private reasons to lie. Tell me everything!" she yelled.

"Monica, stop! Give me a chance to explain."

"What is there to say, other than you are a liar and a thief?"

"For the record, my initial history with Pablo ended a long time ago. After the car crash, I thought that was the end of my dealings with him, and I was relieved beyond measure. I know my hands were not altogether clean, but I was trying to get my life back on track. I was shocked when he contacted me. I knew this would be troublesome and might compromise my relationship with you."

"But you were willing to take that chance? Wow!"

"It was a catch-22. He said I was the only one who could help him."

"So, let me get this straight. As a faithful friend, you chose him over me?"

"Monica, don't look at it like that. Pablo is a dangerous man, and he thinks, for some reason, that I owe him."

"You are a fool! There is no logic in your judgment. And to think we were going to get married. Oh my God! I am the fool!"

"That's not really the way it was. I never wanted to do business with him again, but I could not drop the relationship after he revealed himself. I was dead wrong for thinking I could do this without interrupting our relationship. I should have been honest with you. That would have been fair because you are a good woman. Silly of me to think I could lead a double life. I cheated you, and I don't deserve you."

"Damn straight!"

"I don't have the right to ask for forgiveness, but can you forgive me?"

"Boy, that's a hard ask. If I didn't know Jesus, I probably wouldn't. Still, I need a come-to-Jesus meeting with him."

He grabbed her and hugged her tightly and would not let go. "I need you," he whispered in her ear.

The soothing cadence of his voice exasperated her. She took a deep breath and exhaled slowly. His embrace and the touch of his soft lips on hers erased his conniving ways for the moment. Her decision to let him in was indefensible. They were lost in a temporary moment of love, disobeying every principle of integrity. They moved to the bedroom and lay on the bed, where she cried as they lay in each other's arms.

After a few moments, she asked, "Where have you been?"

"Here, there, but nowhere specifically."

"You have disappointed a lot of people."

"Yes, even myself, but more importantly, you."

"I remembered the day I met you. I saw your arrogance, but

love took over. I am sad to say that the rules of love I trusted are not working for me anymore."

"If it matters any, I want you to know I love you," Ty said, kissing her ear.

Her need to hold onto the moment overruled the unvarnished truth. She wished she could make her feelings go away, but she could not. She ironically felt safe in his strong arms but knew her indulgence was temporary delight and comfort. She fell asleep and woke up hours later to an empty bed.

Ty had vanished. *Like the lyrics to George Benson's song*, she thought.

> *Lovers come and then lovers go*
> *That's what the people say*
> *Don't they know*
> *How it feels when you love me*
> *Hold me and say you care*

Caring is what got her heart in this bind. Only God could get her out now. She dialed Agent Ramos and was thankful the conversation was caught on the bugging device. Just like Grace had said, things were quickly coming to a head.

Two days after Ty's visit, an anonymous check for $75,000 appeared in the Johanssons' Swiss bank account, and seven original paintings arrived via UPS at the Johansson Gallery. Monica knew Ty, in his own way, was trying to make things right. But was it too late?

CHAPTER 50

Retribution

"Colonel, I took care of it, like you asked."

"When?"

"Does it matter, as long as it was done?" Kiko asked with a sneer.

"You've always had a smart mouth."

"Grandfather, you know I got that honestly."

"You are a liar."

"I am?"

"If your father was alive, he would probably slap you, especially for pulling that horrific poisoning stunt. Now, there is blood on our hands. I am seventy-five years old and have no more patience for mistakes like that. You are not the one calling the shots, young lady. Do you understand?"

Kiko did not reply.

Colonel stared her down. "And why are you harassing Grace? What has she done to you?"

Kiko produced a cunning grin.

"That's what I am talking about. I'm concerned about your emotional triggers. Do you have it in you to connect positively to people? I should slap you myself, but I am holding back, waiting for you to change. I taught you martial arts. You know the damage I could do." He held his head down. "Oh, I get it. It is the LAI tool, isn't it?"

Again, Kiko did not reply.

"We have that under control. Salvador drew out the active ingredients, and processing technology and Olu's companies have produced a neutralizing agent with plans to deliver it to our friends for a price. Our scientists have got this. But, Granddaughter, you have to stop acting alone. You seem to have memory lapses. Have you forgotten our plan with Olu? He keeps threatening to quit the operation unless you get your emotions together and put your acting-out in check. It took me a long time to find someone with an aptitude like his to pull off the operation we plan for Pablo. We can't afford to lose him at this critical stage. He's our insurance. Remember, we ultimately want revenge and want our hands to be clean while doing it. So don't mess this up. Also, sometimes we are so unkind to each other because of past mistakes, making the relationships irreparable. We don't want that to happen with Grace."

"But I have done nothing to her."

"Again, you choose to lie to me. What am I to do with you? If only you could have inherited your ancestors' humility." He snorted. "Asahi, your father, was an upstanding businessman who became wealthy by purchasing the artwork of the masters from the Renaissance and Impressionist periods. He was well respected and trusted in the community. He lost millions of dollars when that greedy evil bastard, Azul, took advantage of him as a collector by selling him counterfeit paintings, to be resold to proud Japanese families. Asahi was humiliated and shamed when he found out that he had been fooled. Pablo will pay for his atrocious actions but more for what he did to our people. We will finally be avenged."

Kiko muttered to herself, "I am working on my father's revenge, and you will be proud of me one day."

"Here's my plan." He explained it, finishing with, "Like I said, don't mess it up!"

~

Anonymous Call

"I have a message for Ramos."
"Who's calling?"
"Doesn't matter. I have information about a man and a horse."
"Can you be clearer, ma'am?"
"Do you bet on horses?"
"No, not really."
"Then listen and get this straight," said the strange voice. There's going to be a war at the racetrack."
"Which racetrack?"
"The Kentucky Derby. War Hammer will be there."
"War Hammer? Who is he?"
"Give the message to Ramos."
"Who is this?"
"You are obviously not Ramos. Anyway, be sure to tell him that he will be the lucky winner. The man he wants will be sitting in the owner's section."

Kiko threw the burner phone in a random public garbage bin where it could not be traced.

"Ma'am? Ma'am, what is your name?"

He tried to trace the call to reveal the location, but the call had disconnected.

CHAPTER 51

Girls' Night Out

Pablo watched from the tinted windows of his black Mercedes 300S as Grace and her friends entered their favorite restaurant. His bodyguards routinely had followed Grace on several occasions and knew that Thursday was girls' night out with Ellona and Monica. Pablo entered the restaurant and sat at a back table, waiting until time presented itself to privately confront Grace.

"I'll take two of whatever Ellona's having," Monica said to the waitress.

"Girl, you barely drink a glass of wine. Now you're having two?"

"This issue with Ty is driving me crazy," Monica admitted. "The way Pablo's men beat him was professional and straight out of a gangster movie. As soon as I pulled him into my house, I immediately locked my door and checked to see if anybody was behind him."

"That's some scary stuff. Was that the first time you saw him like that?" Grace asked.

"Yes! You know I would have told you if it had happened before. He has been a businessman up until now," Monica said with an attitude.

"I'm just asking—that's all."

"Whatever went down was not good, and now I'm a nervous wreck. Even though Agent Ramos has somebody watching my house, I still changed the locks on my door, and I'm covering my own back."

"How can you trust him now?" Ellona asked.

"I can't. The good thing is that Agent Ramos captured everything he said on the bugging detector."

"Girl, I'm so sorry this is happening to you. I thought you two were the perfect couple," Grace said.

Monica rolled her eyes.

"Oops, did I say something wrong? My bad. I know I'm the one who persuaded you to see him. I think this is a good time for me to go the restroom before the waitress comes back to take our order. I'll be right back." Grace slowly rose from her seat.

Pablo waited quietly in the dimly lit hallway.

Grace stopped in her tracks when she recognized the faint voice whispering her name. She turned and saw Pablo; she recognized him from the picture Agent Ramos had shared with her. She clamored silently for air.

"Well, if it isn't the artist's wife. You look like you've seen a ghost." He stepped out of the shadows.

"The face has changed, but I know the voice," she said as her adrenaline surged.

He smiled and reached for her. She slapped his hand away.

"You miss me?"

"I thought I was done with you years ago."

"It is good to see you, too. I have been following your impressive career. I always knew you were talented and smart, but you outdid yourself this time. Who would have thought you could create a tool for catching art thieves. You, of all people, a manipulator who forged her own husband's work." He laughed.

"You forced me through blackmail back then, and you know it."

"I didn't have to twist your little arm too far. I think you rather enjoyed it."

"I am not afraid of you, Pablo," she sneered.

"Are you gonna pull a gun on me again?" He laughed.

"If I did, I would not miss. But I am not going to waste my short rage on you. I know, in this season of my life, that you will go down!"

"Still feisty as all get out. Wow! That's sexy."

There was momentary silence.

Grace narrowed her eyes. "What are you doing here, anyway?"

"I needed to see your pretty face up close." He brushed the back of his hand lightly against her cheek.

"Wellington will kill you this time for what you tried to do to me the last time." Grace frowned.

"I have kept my eyes on him too, and we are destined to run into each other one day."

"Are you still involved in illegal art trade?"

"I don't know what you are talking about."

"What you are is a rogue! The facade you've been hiding behind is crumbling."

"We seem to bring out the best in each other," he teased.

"You know this is personal now, don't you?" Grace pointed out.

"Oh, it was personal before. But this time around, you really should be thanking me." Pablo smiled.

"For what?"

"I influenced you to create that tool. If it weren't for me, you would not be rich right now."

"Thank you? I will be thanking God when you are dead!" Grace retorted.

"The old saying goes, 'What doesn't kill you makes you stronger.' I am sure I will see you and your little friend Monica again."

"The only place you'll see me is in your dreams while you are in prison or burning in hell!"

Grace walked away and tried to erase his words, but they echoed in her head. She was shaking on the inside when she returned to her table.

"Who were you talking to in the hallway?" Ellona asked.

"Nobody worth remembering," she replied, trying to calm her ruptured spirit.

Monica realized that Grace was obviously agitated, and Monica did not accept her words as a final answer. "Who was it, Grace?"

Grace reluctantly replied, "Pablo."

"Pablo? Damn! That devil has a lot of nerve showing up here." Monica looked around attentively. "Lord, help us! We need to call Agent Ramos immediately, and you need to call Wellington," She pulled her cell phone out of her purse.

The waitress approached the table, but Grace waved her off.

"Agent Ramos, it's Monica. I'm at a restaurant with Grace and Ellona, and the strangest thing just happened."

"Tell me about it."

"Pablo showed up at the restaurant and cornered Grace when she went to the restroom. She said he also mentioned my name. He obviously has been watching us and followed us here."

"What? Impossible! My men have been following him every day."

"Really? Well, your men need to be fired because they ain't doing a good job."

"What did he say? What happened?"

"I'm not sure, but Grace came back to the table disturbed. She was trying to hide it, but I know her well."

"You ladies need to leave immediately. I will contact Wellington."

"We are leaving the restaurant now, but what about my house? Is it safe for me to go there? Is there any activity going on that I should be aware of?"

"To my knowledge, everything is safe and being monitored. My men have been camped out the entire time. Do you have some other place to stay, or can I get you a hotel for a few days?"

"I have friends I can stay with for a few days, but I need to gather some things from my house first. I hope those aren't the same men who were watching Pablo."

"No, they aren't. As soon as you grab your things, you should leave. I'll let my men know the new plan. Make sure you give me your new address."

"What about Grace? What should she do?" Monica inquired.

"I don't think Pablo is going to go after both her and Wellington. He just wanted to upset her and make an appearance. I think that he is concentrating on something much larger. Have Grace call me when she gets home so I can talk with her and Wellington."

"OK. We are leaving now. Thanks."

Monica, Grace, and Ellona gathered their belongings and headed for the door. She checked their surroundings as they departed.

"Sorry that the mood was altered," Monica said. "Agent Ramos told us to leave immediately. He told me to stay with some friends for a couple of days. Grace, he wants you to call him as soon as you get home. And ladies, please text me once you get home."

"I sure hope Pablo doesn't visit me." Ellona frowned.

"Agent Ramos believes he will not touch any of us. He just wanted to cause some excitement," Monica said.

"If I have the last say, Pablo won't have an opportunity to strike back again. Not on my watch!" Grace exclaimed as the friends exited to their cars.

∼

When Grace arrived home, she and Wellington discussed her encounter with Pablo. They called Agent Ramos, who calmed any worries they had about Pablo reaching out to them. He assured them that his team was monitoring Pablo's whereabouts. He also shared his art crime team's sting mission, which was taking place in two weeks at the Kentucky Derby, where Pablo's horse was competing. He invited them to attend the Derby and witness Pablo's arrest. Agent Ramos thought this was the best way for both Grace and Wellington to have full closure.

After the call, Grace dropped her head and face into her hands, searching for that fearless girl who had fought off the enemy before. The motive *then* was the motive *now*—deliverance and victory! She had promised Radiance that her heroic days were over, but she wasn't sure she could keep her word. The mounting feelings of revenge and retaliation were getting harder to bear and were an understatement of her true feelings. Truth be told, she did not want to be part of the Kentucky Derby sting, but she had to trust Agent Ramos. And God—the job was not too difficult for Him!

CHAPTER 52

Grace's Prayer

"Lord, you know I am grateful for the talents and gifts you have given me. I don't mean to complain, but these seasons in my life are overwhelming, and I am weary from these agonizing challenges and obstacles thrown my way. I need clarity. Why did you choose me to create this tool? These criminals are interrupting my peace and testing my nerves and my faith. My family and friends are terrified, and this is the devil's heyday. I don't deny that my emotions are getting the best of me. I am trying to be a good wife, mother, friend, and artist, but evil surrounds me on all sides. The gravity of the situation is unrelenting. I don't see a clear-cut solution. I am distressed, and I need you to tell me what to do."

Grace had God's attention.

My daughter, give your anxieties to Me. I can handle them. I have the plan for your life. I didn't say it would be easy or that you would understand how all the pieces will fit together. I chose to birth a gift in you that will impact many. Remember—you are fearfully and wonderfully made. This is part of your development in preparation for what you will do in the future. Be assured you are a critical instrument of light. You are exposing darkness, which hates light, and that is why evil is fighting you with all its might. I know your genuine desire for justice. Do not fear! I am with you. Do you remember the words I said to Lazarus's sister Martha? Let Me remind you of John 11:40—"Didn't I tell you if you believe, you will see the glory of God?" I will still the storm to a whisper. Trust Me.

Grace didn't know if she was daydreaming or if she had experienced something supernatural. She felt a shift in her faith, and the determination to triumph over evil.

CHAPTER

53

Calm Before the Storm

On the eve of the Kentucky Derby, Wellington sat on the edge of the bed, rubbing Grace's feet.

"Feels like the calm before the storm," Grace said with a sigh. "We need to enjoy this moment of peace while we can because we don't know what tomorrow will bring."

"Can you believe our boy Ty knew about Pablo?" Wellington asked.

"Poor Monica is a wreck. She has not seen him in a few days."

"That's what a punk does. I would love to get my hands on him and choke the living hell out of him," Wellington said angrily.

"I told Monica she needs to forgive him and leave it in the hands of the Lord. That message is for us, too."

"It is easier said than done. Revenge feels good, but I know it won't accomplish the result we want."

"My nerves are stretched to the limit. I don't know what to expect next," Grace said bleakly.

"Neither of us does. No matter what we are faced with tomorrow, God will not disappoint us."

"That's what keeps a smile on my face." Grace sang and rocked to the words of Kirk Franklin's song "Smile"—"God is working so I smile ... ooo, ooo, ooo."

"You always smile. That's not hard for you."

"That's not always true. My insides are tense this season. I realize I used to be kinder, but all this nonsense has unhinged me and made me rough around the edges. I need to apologize for my short temper and impatience with you." She touched his face gently.

"I understand, dear, but this is not your fault. I know your committed purpose—to bring an end to these illegal art dealings—and that mystery can drain you completely."

"It is working my nerves, for sure. But this foot massage is doing a good job of putting some life back into me." She smiled.

"It makes me so mad that we are in this mess! I thought I didn't have a dog in this fight," Wellington added.

"Oh, but you do, and I think Agent Ramos thought so, too. This has been quite a season, and it is not over. Remember that it is personal, now that Pablo is trying to take advantage of us. He just found another way to do it."

"That ain't happening! God has been on our side, and we will not cave to the pressure. This solidifies why God had you create the LAI tool."

Grace glanced sideways at Wellington. "I want to enjoy life and not always have to fight, but that's part of making a difference in a dark world. Mom told me to push through, and that's what we are going to do."

With a tight smile fixed on his face, Wellington told Grace, "I love you, and I will protect you. Don't let your courage melt away. This is a necessary and relevant season, and you are prepared for the battle. You are a warrior, and we are a warrior family."

Grace squeezed him tightly. "You know what? This could be the best season in my life. I am so blessed to have you at my side. Luther Vandross was right—'You crept into my dreams. When I first met you, I had moments of ecstasy; I slept alone in my fantasy.'"

"So how about pushing through a little fantasy right now?" He pulled her onto the bed, producing a giggle from Grace.

"What are we fantasizing about?"

"Whatever comes to your mind first." He took off his shirt and removed her blouse.

Grace submitted. "OK, I will be part of whatever the artist's appetite is."

"Hey, stay right here."

Wellington breezed down the stairs to his studio and skipped back up with supplies in his hand. He then dropped them at the bedside and said, "I am happy to be your paintbrush."

"Be careful how you blend your colors." She giggled as he touched the small of her back and ran down her spine with a clean paintbrush.

"I got this! Love is what I blend best."

SEASON 9
Defining Moments

CHAPTER

54

Kentucky Derby

On a clear afternoon in the Bluegrass region of Kentucky, Pablo was dressed handsomely in white slacks and a white Fedora. He visited the paddock where his horse, War Hammer, was being saddled and readied for the race. He engaged in lighthearted conversation with the trainer and jockey, Pasqual, before heading to his personal box, where Kiko was seated. In true Kentucky Derby style, she was dressed to impress in a baby blue low-cut lace dress. She wore a matching wide brim hat, complete with a Louis Vuitton handbag and shoes.

Pablo checked the daily racing form, while Agent Ramos, in a covert operation for the arrest, choregraphed a masterful takedown plan. Several of Pablo's many enemies lurked in the grandstands.

"So glad you came." Agent Ramos shook Wellington's hand.

"Grace was hesitant, but you know I would not miss this moment for anything."

"The racetrack is surrounded by the FBI and police officers. It's gonna get real up in here, so stay in your seats. I would not want you to get caught in the crossfire," Agent Ramos advised.

Grace, realizing this was not a made-up moment, gazed nervously at Wellington. She noticed when Kiko, who was seated in a personal box, got up from her seat. She concocted a plan in her head. "I will be right back."

"Where are you going?" Wellington asked, discerning the look on her face.

"To the ladies' room."

"Whatever you are thinking could be counterintuitive. Don't do anything you will regret later."

"I won't."

Grace walked up the few stairs and was several yards behind Kiko when erratic thoughts inundated her mind, causing her to dismiss the idea that brewed like good coffee in her head. It felt like a supernatural nudging by God. The still small voice prompted her to return to her seat.

"That was quick," Wellington observed.

"I decided to be patient and obedient," Grace replied humbly.

"That sounds ambitious." Wellington gave her a wry smile.

Showtime

The post parade began. The horses reached the post position and were in the gates.

"They are off!" the race caller announced. "And down the stretch they go."

The crowd got up on their feet.

"Dapper broke well in front. It is True Blonde breaking right.

Matilde in third. In fifth position is Northern Yankee, followed by Al Chino as they make their way into the clubhouse turn. Into the far turn, toward the inside is Cameo, followed by Jessie on the outside. On the far outside, Cool Breeze is moving up. Miss Tessie is in last. War Hammer is the pacesetter and hitting his stride. Cool Breeze is neck and neck with War Hammer coming into the home stretch. It is coming down to the final sixteenth and down to the wire is—"

Pablo's attention was on his horse, War Hammer, who was in the lead. The crowd roared louder when the horses circled the final lap. He smiled, knowing his biggest purse was moments away. With all the commotion, Pablo did not know that Agent Ramos's team had arrested his men as accessories to a crime, and were coming for him to answer for his old crimes. Kiko nudged Pablo, who looked into his betrayer's eyes, then he turned to his right and saw Ramos in the aisle next to his row. He looked to the left, where two big men blocked the aisle. It all came crashing down.

Kiko jumped over a row of people to escape, losing her heels and hat but not before trying to inflict harm on Grace, spitting a poison dart at her through a straw. It missed but hit a large man in his upper right arm when he jumped in front of Grace and pushed her forward. Kiko fought off three security officers, immobilizing them with her martial arts jujitsu moves before eluding their arrest. She ran under the grandstand and circled back around to aisle two. Pablo was running down the stairway near her.

Pablo's only means of escape was downward, and downward he plunged, into the few stands below, causing a major disruption. He tripped and stumbled and knocked patrons over. With tears streaming down his face, he knew the moment of reckoning was upon him. In an emotional panic and with terror visible on his face, he feared there was no escaping—until he saw Kiko, who signaled to him.

"This way," she said, and he followed. Pablo turned to see who was running after him. The scene was pandemonium. As he turned to face forward again, he ran into the oncoming fast-paced horses. When the horses bucked, the jockeys fell to the ground, Pablo's body was lifted, dropped, then trampled by his own horse. Screams erupted as the noisy and confused crowd witnessed the bloody scene.

Ramos' men ran onto the track to move Pablo's mangled body from harm's way, but it was too late. Pablo was barely holding on. At that moment, as he came to the gory scene, Agent Ramos held a strange compassion for the man he had chased for decades. He called to some of his men to bring water in a futile effort to comfort Pablo in his dying moments.

"Looks like this is the end of the road for you, buddy. You might as well tell me where your base of operation is and where you stashed the money, art, and fraudulent insurance policies."

"Over my dead body." Pablo winced. "If I told you, I'd have to kill you." He coughed and tried to speak. He rattled off some numbers: 5-7-48, 5-1-28, 5-748, which Ramos figured were betting numbers that any gambler might say.

"Life is full of ups and downs." Pablo half smiled. "You must step up." He coughed, and blood dripped profusely from his mouth.

"What do you mean?" Ramos asked Pablo, who was delirious.

"The answer is under your feet," he muttered before taking his last breath.

Grace covered her eyes and fell into Wellington's open arms. He brushed away her falling tears as she witnessed Pablo's sad finale. Grace could not believe that this season for Pablo had come to a horrific and public end.

Kiko dialed the limo to pick her up at Gate Three, Aisle Two. Once she was inside, she took a long, deep breath of relief. She called her grandfather. He owned a fleet of cargo ships that had secret plush living quarters that were used for many situations when it was necessary to lie low and out of sight. They discussed a plan of disappearance for her to the Fiji Islands. He belonged to an organized transnational criminal network, but these vessels were full of cargo.

After speaking with him, Kiko smiled in satisfaction of Pablo's demise and that her family finally got revenge for bringing shame to their name. *I have one last piece of business to attend to*, she thought, *aside from evading Agent Ramos.*

CHAPTER

55

Twist of Fate

Agent Ramos emptied Pablo's pockets and removed his ID before the police arrived. His license revealed a New York address that the FBI team was unaware of. He called his boss to tell him that he would provide a full report, but he knew, first and foremost, he had to get to Pablo's place before anyone else did. He secretly rose early the next morning to catch a flight to New York and listened to the early news as he prepared to leave:

"Breaking news—yesterday, a tragic incident occurred at the Kentucky Derby. As the horses rounded the finish line, a man identified as Pablo Luza, formerly known as Ricardo Azul, was killed when he ran onto the racetrack, into the path of the running horses. It was a gruesome scene beyond anyone's ability to control. One horse had to be euthanized after sustaining severe injuries. Pablo

Luza, reportedly the owner of a participant horse and head of an illegal worldwide art empire, was pronounced dead at the scene. We will follow up with more information on this unfortunate incident at noon. This is Bryon Morris, reporting to you live from Channel 4, NBC News, New York."

Agent Ramos arrived at Kennedy Airport in the early afternoon, rented a vehicle, and drove forty-five minutes to Pablo's Upper West Side Manhattan townhouse, overlooking the Hudson River. The entrance to the condominium was visual proof of Pablo's lavish lifestyle, with its central skylight ceiling and exquisite wood panels. Agent Ramos passed through the hallway and entered a room decorated with a large Persian silk rug and interior walls adorned in soft colors of light blue and gray. A baby grand piano was in the corner, near an open door that led to an office. The office displayed a large bookshelf with a massive collection of books and trinkets. A desk and chairs made of rosewood were located on the left side of the room, which was tastefully lit by a Tiffany lamp on a small round table.

Ramos rummaged through piles of papers on the desk, opened drawers, and shoved several books onto the floor. A small book containing names and betting records fell open. He recalled Pablo's dying words when he had asked him about his raw dealings: "If I told you, I would have to kill you," and then Pablo had rattled off numbers, which Ramos kept in his head. He searched the room for a safe, forcefully thrusting books off the bookshelf until a safe was exposed. Voilà! He barely touched the latch, and it swung open.

Nothing was inside. This was becoming an interesting hunt.

Ramos left the office, entered the hallway, and looked up the winding hardwood staircase. He skipped up, two by two, until he reached the top level. The master bedroom door was open, straight ahead. He entered a beautiful designer white-black-and hazelnut-colored room with a cozy marble fireplace. A large Matisse painting hung over the king-sized bed, encased in the wall. Two matching white chairs faced each other in front of a sixty-inch television located above the fireplace. He checked behind the television to see if there was a wall safe. There was none.

Determined to be thorough, he walked over to the French doors that opened onto an enclosed balcony that overlooked the Hudson River. He opened it and breathed in fresh air before walking back into the room. He entered the orderly walk-in wardrobe closet. It had an integrated shelving system for folded garments, an armoire, and rows of designer suits, shoes, and miscellaneous haberdashery items. He rummaged through the closets but could not locate a safe. He headed back down the stairs, taking them slowly this time. At the last step, he heard a piercing crack.

He stopped at the bottom of the stairs and turned around, recalling Pablo's last words: "You must step up. The answer is under your foot." He turned to the first step, stepped on it again, bent down, jiggled it, and pushed it forward.

It opened into a cubbyhole, and inside lay a safe. He smiled at the cleverly designed hidden compartment where a safe could fit. He tried the numbers Pablo had rattled off playing with it until it opened. He smiled with satisfaction. Inside was a huge stash of cash. He took one of the medium-sized brown sacks he'd brought with him and began filling it to the top. He sat it down on the floor and had turned to retrieve additional money when he was hit over the head with a blunt object. He fell backwards, hitting the side of his head on something sharp. Out of the corner of his eye, he saw Kiko before he passed out.

She hadn't known of his talent to snatch information with a quick glance, but Kiko was one step ahead of Agent Ramos. She had a key to Pablo's place and had arrived moments before he did to do her own search, but she was interrupted when she heard a key turn in the door. She had hidden quietly and waited until the right time to strike.

"You ばか [fool]!" She laughed wickedly as she gathered the goods that scattered across the floor. She placed them in a brown sack and joyfully dragged it across the hardwood floor. She lifted it into a large black suitcase and wheeled it to her new Mercedes Benz which was hidden in the garage. She lifted the suitcase into the trunk; traveled across the George Washington Bridge into New Jersey, listening to the jazz greats for miles before stopping at a New Jersey Turnpike rest stop.

In her exhilaration from killing a high-ranking law official, she opened the bag and pulled out several stacked Hamilton bills. She recalled that Pablo always had bragged about his massive earnings that he kept in a safe because he didn't trust banks. She was livid. This appeared to be only a small fraction of his fortune. She was the fool now! The plan for the South Pacific was now an inevitable necessity.

Recovery

Agent Ramos pushed himself up from the hard floor and held his battered head. It took him a few moments to realize what had happened. The last thing he recalled was getting hit over the head and seeing Kiko at his side. He noticed small traces of money scattered across the floor and rushed to the safe. He swung the stair open. *Damn it!* She had gotten the rest. He sat on the stairs in disgust. That's when Pablo's additional last words came to him: "Life is full of ups and downs." He aggressively searched the second step, and it opened, as did the third, and then the fourth. Just like the first step, all were masterfully built and had a cubbyhole with a safe inside. In spite of his throbbing head, he shouted for joy.

The second step contained the insurance papers and betting scores, and the third and fourth, tons of cash. He smiled to himself. After looking over the insurance papers, he observed the various insurance payouts to Pablo. He dialed his boss, Amare Jackson, to report the good news of the cash and evidence that he was able to recover, but realized he would receive a harsh tongue-lashing for launching out on his own again—and for not having a warrant to enter Pablo's home. He knew contacting Jackson meant getting chewed out again.

CHAPTER

56

The Long and Short of It

Grace, Wellington, and Agent Ramos listened silently as a TV anchorman spoke.

"Salvador Franco, thirty, a portrait painter from Milan, Italy, philanthropist Tyler Hamilton, age forty, from Berkeley Heights, Switzerland, and Olu Adebayo, age forty-one, from New York City, pled guilty to federal criminal charges in an elaborate scheme to defraud art dealers and collectors out of millions of dollars. The FBI Art Crime Task Force announced today that it's trying to identify the rightful owners of more than one hundred paintings seized in a New York sting raid related to this case. If you have any information connected to this matter, contact us at NBC.com. More news on this story at eleven. This is Bryon Morris, reporting live from Channel 4, NBC News, New York."

"Agent Ramos, congratulations on a job well done." Wellington grinned.

"We owe you," Grace agreed.

"An ending like this makes it all worth it. I am glad to finally have Pablo off the streets, posing no further threat to all of you. I am happy that your paintings were recovered. I will get some rest as soon as I catch the girl who took a bat to my head at Pablo's house." He smiled as he took off his black hat to rub his head.

CHAPTER 57

The Valinda Daniels Show

The seating arrangement for the top cultural-arts television show in Times Square in New York was circular, with a white low table in the middle of the floor and white high-back chairs. Valinda Daniels, Grace, and Dr. Monica Wolf took their seats and made final adjustments before the cameraman put up his fingers to countdown.

"Welcome, friends, to our show, *Inside the Big Picture*," Valinda said. "Today, our guests are Grace Holmes, author, inventor, wife, mother, entrepreneur, and the creator of the Liquid Art Intelligence, or LAI, tool; and Dr. Monica Wolf, a microscopy researcher at the Centers for Disease Control. Welcome, ladies. We are blessed to have you on our program.

"Thank you," Grace and Monica said in unison.

"Grace, congratulations on the Liquid Art Intelligence tool that is making big waves in the international art world."

"Thank you. The results exceeded our modest expectations. I am humbled by the opportunity to create a solution for change."

"I see you brought along a sample product."

Grace nodded and held up the shapely bottle that was similar in size to a perfume spray bottle.

"That's a cute little bottle with a lot of power," Valinda said. "Tell us its function and how it works."

"It acts as an aerosol spray," Grace said. "I cannot share the trade secret, but I will say that with an application and the use of a certain light spectrum, the authenticity of a piece of artwork is identified."

"How unique. What prompted you to create this?"

"It was born of necessity to reduce increased levels of art theft. Most artists selling expensive artwork are alarmed by the proliferation of replicas. Valinda, I know that you have heard the phrase, 'Necessity is the mother of invention.'"

"Yes, I have."

"Art theft is a huge criminal enterprise with annual losses in the billions," Grace explained. "A tool like this will aid in penetrating criminal activity."

"You mentioned that the idea was conceived in a dream. Am I correct?"

"Yes. It was an active dream. As soon as I woke up, the idea was sealed in my spirit, and I shared it with my husband, Wellington. We both knew that it was worth a try to see if it was a solution to art theft."

"Was it an aha moment?" Valinda asked.

"Exactly. A very inspired aha moment. I felt a keen awareness of God's presence. I presented it to my team, and it took a long time to develop, do trials, file the paperwork, and market the product. But it was worth the wait. I want to give a shout-out to Wellington and to

Monica for their support and for keeping me sane during the long development process."

"It is important to have people in your corner who believe in you. I understand you have a great team and other ladies behind you as well."

"I call them my Angel Squad. Dr. Monica Wolf is a gifted scientist, and my technical team of Tracey Vinson and Georgie Houston are bright, young, innovative engineers. Together, we were able to develop a special item. We all are members of the Artist Wife Organization. I believe we are given gifts to make a difference and to find solutions to problems."

"Dr. Wolf," Valinda said, turning in Monica's direction, "Congratulations on the great work you are doing at the CDC as an autoimmune disease specialist. Tell me how you got involved in the LAI project."

"Grace and I share a passion for justice in the art world. My deceased husband was an artist, so teaming up with Grace was a no-brainer. It is rewarding to be part of this project."

"Grace, from a museum standpoint, what is the impact of LAI on international and state museums?" Valinda asked.

"Thus far, we have received many positive reports from museums. Before it hit the various markets, there was no way to identify the owner of great works of art from a replica in the manner that this tool does."

"Are there really no other methods out there?"

"There are a few but nothing of this nature, where you can determine the authenticity immediately."

"How many stolen art items are actually recovered or returned to the rightful owners?"

"Out of the million works of art stolen each year, only 10 percent are recovered and returned. This tool will greatly impact that percentage."

"Thank you, ladies. Tell me more about the Artist Wife Organization. How did you get started?"

"Back in the day, there were only a few of us who traveled the art circuit to support our husbands or significant others at art exhibits," Grace said. "Over the years, our bond of friendship grew."

"Grace had the passion and the purpose," Monica explained. "She saw an opportunity for us to talk to each other about our supportive roles as spouses. We strengthened one another through discussions and realized how other artists' wives could benefit from this type of camaraderie."

"Over the years, we grew in numbers, and last year we held our first West Coast seminar in Los Angeles." Grace said. "It was a huge success."

Valinda smiled. "I'm going to look into joining this group myself. I too am married to a creative person. I could use some therapy right now."

They laughed.

Valinda looked at her notes and then said, "Grace, I read about the recent tragedy at the Kentucky Derby. A man who was involved in illegal art trade was run over by his own horse. I don't want to dwell on it, but I heard that you and he had some history, and that he is the wicked character in your husband's new movie, 'The Wellington Holmes Story'. Can you touch on how that affected your life?"

Grace braced herself before answering. "It was a crazy, unbelievable swing of events that led up to that day." Her voice cracked, and she had to steady herself again. "I have to thank God for the lessons learned in each season of my life. There is a deeply emotional backstory that I can't explain right now. But I will say this: Pablo Luza, the man who was killed, was running a corrupt art empire that affected the entire international art community. There were multiple challenges in trying to take him down. What is so interesting is that things did not work out at first like I thought they would. We sometimes think we have closure on a matter, until something happens that blows that theory out of the water. I was so angry. I admit I had evil thoughts about him and had to repent."

Valinda nodded. "I think all of us have had to get our anger in check on one occasion or another. Am I right about it?"

They nodded their heads in unison, and Grace said, "Dr. Martin Luther King, Jr. said in one of his speeches, 'Let justice roll on like a river, righteousness like a never-failing stream.' We believe justice was served."

"I'll bet that this time around, there is a sweet and lasting victory," Valinda said.

Grace smiled. "Yes ma'am."

"Thank you. If you want to learn more about the Artist Wife Organization, the contact information is located at the bottom of the screen. Ladies, thank you for your contribution to the arts. I wish you the best in your future projects."

"Thank you for having us," Grace said.

Monica smiled in agreement. "It was a pleasure to appear on *Inside the Big Picture*."

Relieved that the interview was over, Grace returned to the green room, while Monica stopped and chatted with Valinda. Grace was surprised to find a large vase of beautiful orchids sitting on the table. She wondered who had sent this arrangement.

She tore open the handwritten note. Her demeanor immediately changed, and fear tried to rip through her heart as she read the message:

> Artist wife girl, you should be thanking me for rescuing you from Pablo, a thorn in all of our sides. It has been said that the only constant thing in life is change. I cannot wait until the next season starts. Yours to the end!
>
> 喝采 [Cheers]!
> Kiko

Grace felt a tightness in her throat. The audacity of Kiko, taking a bow as the hero! Imagine that! Despite Kiko's bad—or were they good?—intentions, Grace crumbled the note and violently threw the flowers into the trash, refusing to allow the intrusion to emotionally sway her vision. Then, she remembered her mission and thought about her impulsiveness. She quickly gathered the flowers and placed them back in the vase and retrieved the note from the trash as evidence for Agent Ramos. She thought about her mom, and a chord was struck that her courage and her faith would not be diminished.

She reflected on her mother's words—"Every trial is a blessing in your refinement." She could feel her face flush as she wrote a response to Kiko on a nearby napkin which she could transfer on paper later.

> Kiko, girl, it is a new season in which I realize my difficult moments are behind me. God's steadfast protection shaped my seasons, and now my defining moment is turning the page. Nobody, not even you, will deter me or impede my journey.

Artist Wife

~

Radiance stood in the Green Room doorway, observing the blank look on her mother's face. "What beautiful flowers," she said, interrupting Grace's thoughts as she entered the room.

"Yes, they are." Grace greeted her with a warm hug.

"Dad has great taste."

Wellington walked in and saw the flowers. "They are beautiful, but I didn't send them. Javier called and said he needed some money. Maybe he sent them."

Grace held the torn note tightly in her hand, not wanting to open a new season of fear. She decided to stretch the truth. "They're from an artistic competitor to apologize for her bad behavior. I'm not planning on seeing her anytime soon," she said firmly.

"Mom, you were great in the interview," Radiance said, beaming. "I'm so proud of you. You are my hero."

"Baby girl, I'm just a normal person who wants to do the right thing. I have to apologize to you, though, because I told you I wouldn't be that warrior woman again—and I wasn't, entirely," Grace admitted.

Wellington smiled. "Yes, but up to the end of things, you certainly tried. Remember that you jumped out of your seat at the Kentucky Derby when all the commotion started with Pablo." He turned to Radiance. "But I held her back. Because I have her back."

"I guess she just has it in her blood to fight back," Ruth said as she entered the room.

"Mom!" Grace grinned, as she ran toward her mom's embrace. "You know I was always shy."

"Yes, you were. But your dad wasn't. I can't take credit for the bold young lady you've become."

"I'm just thankful that you always have a listening ear and shoulder to lean on. If it wasn't for the prayer warrior you are, where would I be? I love you so much." Grace hugged her again.

"Granny, thank you for being here for me too," Radiance added. "Family is everything."

"Speaking of family, where are Ellona and Monica?" Grace asked.

"Did I hear somebody mention our names?" Ellona peeked into the doorway of the Green Room, with Monica right behind her.

"Ladies, get in here." Grace urged them forward with her hands. "Yes, we were talking about you." Grace smiled. "Thanks, ladies, for supporting my family and my vision. Most of all, thank you for being the best friends a girl could have."

"We wouldn't have it any other way," Monica said.

"Girl, you have to stop having all the fun by yourself. Promise me that you will let me in next time." Ellona laughed. "In fact, I can't wait to see what is next."

"Next? Are you kidding me? Definitely none of the nonsense we experienced in these last few seasons." Grace exhaled a sigh of relief.

"The next thing we are going to do—as a family, right here, right now—is celebrate!"

"That's right," Wellington said. He broke open the bottles of champagne and poured it in glasses, except for Radiance who received orange juice.

"And then I'm going on a vacation and spending some quality time with my entire family," Grace said.

"That sounds good to me." Wellington placed a soft kiss on Grace's lips. "I'm thankful to God that these seasons are over and for taking care of my family. Group hug!" he shouted.

They closed in together and toasted.

"Now, what were you saying about that vacation?" Wellington whispered to Grace. "When do we leave?"

CHAPTER 58

Season's End

"Radiance, hurry up. Javier is waiting for us on the Zoom call," Grace said.

"Yes, Mom!" Radiance called from her room, "I'm finishing up my assignment. I'll get on Zoom in a minute."

Grace turned to face the screen and saw Javier. "Hey, sweetheart."

"Hey, Mom."

Grace loved when he called her *Mom*. It was endearing and confirmed their closeness and the bond they had built since his mom died several years ago. She grew sad for a moment, thinking how his birth mom could not witness his many accomplishments.

"How's school, son?" Wellington said, entering the room and taking a chair next to Grace.

"Hey, Dad. It's so cool. I'm really enjoying it and bonding with the brothers."

"Just the brothers?" Wellington said with raised eyebrows. "I seem to recall the most important sweet ingredient that walked the halls was the ladies."

Javier laughed. "Yes, Dad, they are hard to ignore, for sure. Some real beauties and smart women are here on campus. I swear they must have gathered all the fine women in the world and placed them at Howard." He smiled.

Radiance joined the Zoom call from her bedroom. "Hey, Javier. What's up?"

"Hey, lil sis. I'm good."

Wellington laughed. "I think he's better than good."

"Did I miss something?" Radiance asked.

"Nah. Dad's just teasing me about the ladies."

"How do you like college?" Radiance asked. "And when can I come to visit?"

"It's super cool. Right now, we are just coming out of COVID-19, but things are safe here. The vaccine is finally reaching the campuses, and many students are deciding whether to take it or not. It's a big discussion. But overall, I'm loving college and adjusting to classes and to the DC area. I'm coming home in a couple of weeks, and we can talk about a visit then."

"Cool. We're taking a family vacation when you come."

"Guys, during the vacation, we want to talk with you about the seasons we just came through," Grace said. "It wasn't easy. We know you had to make many sacrifices, and we did too. We thank you for that and for your prayers."

"Mom, I don't know what to say," Javier said, "other than I hope you and Dad are OK. You went through a lot and handled your business."

"Your dad and I pressed through this long season of evil activities. As we stayed on course, God had a breakthrough for us, on course with what we believed and hoped to obtain, which is change for the art community. Seasons will come, and they will go. But whatever you do, *stay the course*. Stay the course with school, Javier, and Radiance, stay true to your passion. Even in the darkest of times, God is always with us and will be with you, too. We're good."

"Son, these seasons have tested our family, our fortitude, our patience, and our faith. I know we all have been stressed, juggling family, business, and school. But know that our first priority is to you two. We promise to protect you, to support you, and, most of all, to love you. That will never change. Even before I knew your dad, my mother's words of encouragement over the years have been the glue that held me together and kept me in the lowest of times. That is what I want to be for you two."

"And the same goes for me, Javier," Wellington added. "You don't have to be a lone soldier now that you're away from home. Call me sometime. Stay in touch. We can continue building our relationship, and you and Radiance have the same opportunity, as well. It is important that we keep family first."

"Like the apostle Paul said in 1 Corinthians 9:24, our goal is to run a race, that we may obtain the prize. So, it's all about how you run your race," Grace said softly. "We may have stepped into deep territory since creating the LAI, but when you believe strongly in something, you run into uncanny undertakings. That happened based on an incredible idea that God gave me. We are human and don't have all the answers, but we do have faith and have to exercise it. That's all we can go on. This was a big test for all of us. Your dad supported my idea, and the team developed a necessary product. We had no idea it would cause such a commotion and uncover a dangerous character—one we thought was already taken care of."

"The bottom line is that the victory we obtained is sweet and the goal continues—to live and leave a legacy that will impact lives and make a difference in the community," Wellington added.

"Dad and Mom, I'm so proud of you," Javier said.

"Yes, I agree with Javier. Thanks for the heartfelt talk. We appreciate you more than you know," Radiance added.

"We love you, too," Grace said.

"We're looking forward to seeing you in a few weeks to go on vacation and celebrate your first semester," Wellington said. "Believe me, it will be a fresh season that we all can look forward to."

Their conversation was interrupted by the sound of the garage door opening. Their hearts raced as Wellington and Grace quickly glanced at one another. Wellington jumped from his chair in the upstairs bedroom and looked out the front window just in time to see a slender figure wearing a black hoodie and black sweats. The intruder ran from the side of Grace's Mercedes, jumped over the fence, and disappeared into the trees. How could this be? They lived in a secure gated community.

Wellington took the winding stairs two by two, landing squarely on his feet. He grabbed his .357 Smith & Wesson Magnum from the hallway closet and motioned to Grace to keep Radiance at the top of the stairs. He raced out the front door and cautiously approached Grace's open car door. The pulled down sun visor on the driver's side displayed the garage door opener and on the seat was a large manila envelope. The intruder obviously wanted to get their attention.

Wellington closed the car door and then noticed Grace standing in the front doorway. He quickly ran to the side fence, but the intruder was long gone. Entering the backyard, he checked the perimeter of the property and the back door, but he saw no one. He circled back to the front of the house and met his perplexed wife at the doorway.

Wellington re-entered the house, brushing past Grace as he tore open the envelope. A photo of Javier fell out, showing him sitting in his class at Howard University. Several rows behind him on the left sat an individual wearing a baseball cap and dark glasses. Wellington's blood pressure rose as he read the note aloud: *From where I sit at Howard University, things are pointing to a great new season. I can't wait!* Wellington's hand dropped to his side. Grace grabbed the note and noticed it was unsigned. "Can you believe this! Wellington exclaimed. "The nerve! We ain't having this...!" Grace erupted.

Grace refused to be defined by a spiteful delusional perception of her next season. She didn't need to prove anything to anyone. She fixed her mind on the truth and was determined to reply on God's grace and peace.

This was a pivotal moment in Grace's seasons. That was then ... this is now!

> Don't be weary in well doing, for in due season, you will reap if you faint not.
>
> —Galatians 6:9